Other books by Tim W. Nordberg:

Adult Reading
Hijacking of One-Three Juliet
Three-One Juliet
The Legend of Maryna
The Legend of Maryna: The Tsars Lost Gold

Children's Books
The Adventures of Juliet the Airplane
The Adventures of Pixie and Ella: The Big Outdoors

Six Miles Above the Earth

Tim W. Nordberg

Six Miles Above the Earth

Tim W. Nordberg
Copyright © 2020
All Rights Reserved

AUTHOR'S NOTE

This book is a work of fiction. Names, Characters, places and incidents are products of the author's imagination or are used fictitiously. Any resemblance to actual events or locales or persons, living or dead, is entirely coincidental.

The scanning, uploading and distribution of this book via the internet or any other means without the written permission of the publisher is illegal and punishable by law. Please purchase only authorized electronic editions, and do not participate in or encourage electronic piracy of copyrighted materials. Your support of the author's rights is appreciated.

No part of this publication may be reproduced in whole or in part without the written permission of the publisher. For information regarding permission, please email

Timwnordberg@gmail.com

Airline Note:
This book contains a fictional U.S. based airline, Nor'Easter Airlines. It is a fictional book, with standard references used in the airline world, but not tied to one specific airline or set of procedures.
All evidence of philosophy, references, routes and airplane equipment has been fabricated for dramatic effect, and bear no resemblance or relation to any U.S. flagged airline operating in the past or at the time of this publication.

To my wife Alia, who exemplified doing things right versus quickly,

and

To my daughter Grace, may she know that she can achieve anything she puts her mind to.

ACKNOWLEDGEMENTS

To the artists, editors and airline professionals who guided me through the challenging maze of producing this novel, thank you!

I would especially like to recognize the following individuals/companies:

Book Cover:
Blake Pieck from
Valour Of Writing
www.valourofwriting.net
Blake, thank you for developing a world-class book cover. I've had a lot of wonderful compliments regarding the cover!

Editors:
Debbi Shibuya from
My Debstinations
Mydebstinations.me
Debbi, you've helped me edit several books now, and I'm extremely happy with how they turned out. You're a great partner!

Madi Johnson
Madi, thank you for taking your time in helping me perfect this book in so many ways. You've got an incredible talent and I'm truly grateful for your skills and your support! I look forward to hearing your feedback in my books to come!

I wrote Six Miles Above the Earth during the COVID-19 quarantine. It was written as a way to "unplug" from the politics and economical impacts of recent events.

There are several big takeaways I wanted to highlight in this book.

The first illustrates the professionalism of our pilots during the trying times of decreased air travel and the airline industry. They, along with healthcare, military, and law enforcement workers, are *essential* for a reason.

The second highlight is even bolder. I wanted to recognize that we are living in an age where we have greater focus on our veterans and veteran suicide from various reasons.

Our veterans have seen a lot of humanity over the years of war, to include being face to face with enemies who want to kill them. We owe our veterans the dignity and respect to get the help they need in order to return to a "normal" life after what they've seen and done. Remember the 22 per day.

   -Tim W. Nordberg

Prologue

At a hotel just outside of New York's LaGuardia airport
04:30 a.m.

An early morning light filtered into the dimly lit hotel room as the air conditioning unit's compressor rattled on, blowing icy cold air around the blinds and gently jostled them, giving the room a subtle glow. Along with the movement of the blinds, their clicking sound knocking together interrupted the slumber of the only two occupants in the room. The humidity in the room slowly evaporated as the temperature cooled.

The silky-smooth naked body of a petite but well-defined, fit body wrapped around Captain Mitchell Bordoux. Her butt was firm, tight, and the perfect kind of round. Her legs were muscular and toned. Her un-supported breasts were smaller but perky, and the perfect size that complemented her small frame. They were a physical feature that Mitch very much enjoyed about his lover.

Mitch's sexual attention was redirected by the rattling of the hotel blinds, which had startled the two lovebirds from their "sleep," after a night of passionate sex.

Jenny had been a five-year flight attendant with the small regional airline. She enjoyed the job, but she had higher aspirations of becoming a flight attendant at a mainline airline or even "crossing over to the dark side" and eventually becoming a pilot for the same airline she worked for.

Jenny was the kind of person who never really planned things through in their entirety. She loved to travel and loved the adventure of being in a different city each night.

Jenny was a busy flight attendant, and some of the trips became very routine, with the exception to this trip. What made this trip so wonderful was she had been able to fly with her private captain, and the trips were not so overly exhausting with requirements that ended up pushing the crew against their mandatory off-duty rest cycles at the end of each day.

On the other hand, Mitch was a seven-year airline transport-rated pilot who had managed to upgrade from the right seat to captain about two years prior.

Once he received his captain wings, he joined the ranks of selected pilots in an instructor program within the airline, helping to train and develop the next generation of new-hire airline pilots. The program was a challenging one, but it was well-built and allowed select pilots to shine above the rest when it came time for the majors to start recruiting them.

In addition to the airline gig, Mitch also served part-time in the military as a Technical Sergeant in the Ohio Air National Guard. Nobody really talked to him about it, and he didn't offer much information about this. His job, through his words, was pretty mundane.

Mitch had flown for the regional airlines for several years, but recently, since his application was rejected by a major U.S. air carrier, he really began thinking about what his future held.

In an attempt to change course in his military life, Mitch applied to become a fighter pilot, which had also been one of his longtime dreams. Just two months ago, Mitch interviewed for a pilot position at the Ohio Air National Guard base, which housed F-16 Fighting Falcon jets.

Captain Mitch, as people liked to call him, had a reputation with the ground crews that he wasn't very empathetic towards their causes. He used to make statements like, "I did a lot more and got paid less than you when I was overseas," which seemed to marginalize complaining crew members.

Mitch's military career was entirely in a career field called air transportation, which was basically the movement of cargo and passengers to and from arriving/departing aircraft. He was proud to be a "Port Dawg," though nobody really knew or asked what that meant or what the significance of that name really was.

When down range, he loved the adventure of being the first boots in and the last boots out. He had been deployed several times to countries like Qatar and Afghanistan, where he saw some pretty dysfunctional aspects of war, even inside the wire.

Jenny was a veteran as well. She had enlisted in the Marine Corps when she was 17, under the approval of her parents. She went to basic training and technical training immediately after graduating from high school in New Jersey. Shortly after she had arrived to her duty station in South Carolina, her unit was advised to prepare for a combat tour in the Middle East, on relatively short notice.

From the very beginning, Jenny armed up and worked just as hard as the men that she worked next to, eventually gaining their respect as their equal. She was known to be a hard-ass. She needed to be, in order to conform to military life and "measure up" to the rest of the men, especially in a warzone.

Reality set in as Jenny's attention shifted to the night stand, where her phone buzzed and illuminated the immediate area with a soft blue hue. It was face-down, but imperfections on the table allowed the light to escape from her outdated iPhone. The buzzer went off, which alerted the couple that it was time to get ready for their day of work. It was night three of their four-day trip.

After turning off the alarm, Jenny braced her arms on the bed and pushed her upper torso up and off Mitch's chest, allowing her firm breasts to hang and then drag and tickle his chiseled hairless chest.

Mitch gave out an audible exhale as he sighed and stretched, thinking of the last time he felt so complete. It had been a long time since he had that feeling of being whole.

"Shit," Jenny softly whispered, her arms collapsing, allowing Mitch's chest to bear the full weight of her toned and light-framed body. She exhaled as she brushed her long chestnut brown hair from her eyes, and laid her head back down on his chest, wishing that she didn't have to get up.

Jenny's hair dangled in Mitch's face, and it was the most pleasant smell that really gave him a sensual feeling in the pit of his stomach.

"It's time to get up," Jenny whispered into Mitch's ear, knowing the very moment she called it quits would inevitably mean a cry for one more round "for the road."

Mitch looked at his watch, and it showed precisely 4:32 a.m. "Let's call in sick," Mitch said quietly, conspiring to allow the two of them some more alone time.

Jenny smirked and shook her head, rejecting the whole idea.

"C'mon," Mitch cried out softly, his bottom lip hanging out like a pouty little boy. "Okay, instead of calling in sick, maybe just one more time?" Mitch pleaded like a little boy begging with his mother to read him another bedtime story.

Jenny snickered at the whole scenario that she had just foretold in her head. And, just as she had thought, she was the one who had to finalize a decision.

"Oh, Mitch, you know the rules…" Jenny smiled innocently. "When it's time for business and being a professional, we agreed there would be no debate," she said, playfully scolding Mitch for pleading for one more act of coitus before getting up and getting ready for another busy day in the office.

Mitch scrunched his face in fake disappointment as he protested, "That's for when we're already dressed and six miles above the earth."

Mitch had worked with some pretty stunning women in the airline, but he never thought about dating or marrying someone from his work. It was too dangerous if things didn't work out. Jenny was different, though. She had the same work *and* off-work values as he did.

She was everything that, in his mind, he pre-determined would be the exception to every co-worker dating rule ever made… even wife material.

Mitch glanced down at his aroused self, somewhat sad and let down, and then looked back up at Jenny as she sat up and re-situated her naked self, sitting on the soft pit of his stomach.

Jenny reached over, gently sliding her soft and tame hand across Mitch's fit chest, debating on which decision she was going to make. While thinking, she pinched her bottom lip with her teeth, putting more effort into her decision.

"Fuck," Jenny said softly as she exhaled. She wanted it too, but she also needed to get ready for work. The great debate in her mind was about which of the options was deemed more important at that time. It was a challenging dilemma.

Jenny grew up in a military family. Her father served in the 1980s, 1990s, and throughout the Gulf War as a Marine. Her mother was a Navy nurse, and all of her uncles had also served in various capacities.

These strong traits really pushed Jenny's belief in how she lived life in a different light. She was tough, because she *knew* she had no other choice. She always persevered. It's just the type of person she was.

In the military, both Jenny and Mitch knew the consequences of being late due to their own accord. There was strict accountability that had been engrained into both of them, and it was strictly believed that if you were not early, you were already late. In the civilian world, however, and with an airline, as long as you showed up for your flight on time, nobody said anything.

Jenny looked over at Mitch, who proceeded to give her puppy dog eyes, trying everything in his male-wired toolbox to get another round of pleasure before starting their busy workday.

"Look, we don't depart until 7:30, it's a five-minute ride from here to the terminal. We have time for one more quick round," Mitch persisted and pleaded with a gentleman's smile, hoping that'd do the trick.

"Oh, babe, I know, but I need to get ready so you can get ready, captain," Jenny said softly.

"This isn't drill weekend; we aren't pressed for time. We will be just fine. Besides, *I* am the captain now," Mitch said smiling, making a joke off a Tom Hanks movie.

Jenny chuckled at the movie reference. She always loved the cheesy movie references that Mitch came up with, especially at the most inopportune times. It's what really turned her on. Jenny took in a deep breath and dipped her head before she finally caved into the request.

"You're a very bad role-model," Jenny said, smiling and digging her index finger into Mitch's chest as she resituated herself again.

"Am I?" Mitch asked as he rolled Jenny on her back and climbed on top of her.

Before long, the two had finished, and Jenny got up from the bed and excused herself in order to jump into the shower and expedite the process of getting ready for work.

Mitch sat up from the bed and glanced over at his luggage. There was a slight bulge in one of the front pockets. He got to his feet, his stomach feeling tense as he retrieved the beautiful engagement ring that had been sitting untouched, waiting to be presented.

After Mitch spent a few moments looking at it, he put it back in the security of the pouch, making sure that it was safe and secure.

While putting his gift back into his flight bag, a letter was taunting him to open it. It was an official letter from the United States Air Force, and it was formally addressed to Technical Sargent Mitchell Bordoux.

Mitch had waited until the right moment to open it when he could celebrate or be let down with the love of his life.

Either way, he strongly believed that Jenny would be there as his wife-to-be.

The envelope was thin, and didn't have a whole lot of weight behind it. Mitch had his suspicions, but finally, curiosity got the best of him and he opened his letter.

The letter was pretty straight forward. It began formally, as most other official communications from the government had.

Mitch read the words until he reached the one line he was dreading, "We regret to inform you that you have not been selected for Undergraduate Pilot Training."

A sinking feeling overcame him, as well as a strong desire to find out what he could have done differently in the interview process.

While waiting for his turn in the bathroom, Mitch went back to bed and laid down as his head hung in defeat.

He glanced over at his phone, which was plugged in on the night stand next to the window. He picked up the phone and started scrolling through his social media before he suddenly got interrupted by the sound of another buzzing tone, one that he hadn't recognized before. Two minutes later, the phone buzzed again.

Curious of what was buzzing (and where), Mitch got out of bed again, the cold air blowing past his lower extremities and causing a cool reaction of clenching his stomach muscles. He went over to where his flight bag was, and where Jenny sprawled out her suitcase, and he moved around a couple of the bags when another phone was found lying face-up, displaying the first line of several text messages.

Puzzled as to why Jenny would have another phone, Mitch reached down and picked up the phone and scrolled through the four text message previews on the lock screen.

Mitch's stomach suddenly tied itself into a large knot. His confusion quickly turned into an almost out-of-body experience where his blood boiled.

Mitch took a deep breath in, putting the phone back down where he found it. His mind was raw and overwhelmed with twisted emotions as he stood motionless, thinking for a second.

Looking down at the two bags, Jenny's stuff intermixed with his, he began picking up all his articles in an effort to expedite the checkout process and evade the current situation as quickly as he could.

It wasn't long after Mitch packed the bags, leaving the basic essentials, that Jenny emerged from the bathroom, the steam permeating like a fog bank coming ashore. The floral smell of shampoo and body wash followed Jenny as she left the bathroom. Her hair was wrapped up in one of the hotel's complimentary white towels, and another larger towel was wrapped around her body.

"It's all yours, Captain," Jenny said, smiling innocently.

Mitch forced a smile and walked into the bathroom. He passed by Jenny without saying a word, shut the door behind him, and ran the shower.

These sorts of trips weren't abnormal for the regional airline crews. It wasn't unheard of to be on three or four-day trips, bouncing around the eastern United States in small 76-seat jets.

Jenny finished her prep items, making sure that she was presentable and that everything was perfect.

One thing about Mitch was that he expected proper dress and appearance, as that was part of their job to present customers with a professional appearance. The company sold a service, and it was up to him and all other captains to enforce the rules while onboard company aircraft. After all, the customers paid their wages.

When Jenny finished collecting her things and packed them into her compact roller duffle, she took one more look around the bed and nightstand. Satisfied that she didn't forget anything, she rolled her mini suitcase out into the hallway of the hotel and began making her way towards the elevator bank. She didn't have far to walk, as the elevators were just a couple of doors down from her room.

The hotel had a trademark scent. It always smelled fresh and they had the same scent, no matter which location the crew would visit. It was always a relaxing feeling, almost like beach air wafting from the Florida beaches.

Satisfied that she was prepped for work and was able to meet the standards of her boss, she pressed the elevator call button. Just as she released her finger from the button, she looked around and came face-to-face with her cohort: another flight attendant, Wanda, who had gone through training with Jenny a few years ago.

It was this trip that they were paired together as cabin crew for the first time in several months, but never on a multi-day trip. It was a nice change of pace, since they were rarely able to work together. This was a shame, since they always enjoyed each other's company, especially when it came to talking about boys.

"Good morning, Wanda," Jenny smiled innocently as Wanda approached the elevators with her luggage in tow.

Wanda smiled while she gave Jenny a thorough once-over. "Good morning, where's Prince Charming at?" she asked in her typical New York accent.

Jenny's eyes shot over to Wanda nervously, hoping that she didn't figure out the secret code of conduct between her and Mitch.

"No such thing," Jenny chuckled. She looked back from the hotel room that she had exited, hoping that nobody really caught a glimpse of her leaving a room that wasn't assigned to her.

"Shame," Wanda replied, chuckling a tired laugh.

"Didn't sleep well?" Jenny asked, noting the tired look and bags under Wanda's eyes.

"No, never do, especially after coming back from vacation," Wanda half-smiled.

The elevator doors opened, and inside stood a perfectly-groomed gentleman in a pilot uniform with three gold stripes attached to his shoulders, along with a jacket draped over his flight roller bag.

The man stood a little over 5'6" and had a thin frame, but with strong, square shoulders. The pilot uniform and jacket sat nicely on his fit frame.

His head was shaven and had a clean sheen to it. In contrast to his head, he had a mustache that resembled the infamous Robin Olds, who was a Vietnam fighter ace.

Jim was a middle-aged Chicago resident. The wedding ring on his finger told the tale that he was a family man.

He recently joined the airlines in a spur-of-the-moment mid-life crisis, which took him away from his previous occupation (I.T. and banking). He had been a commercially rated pilot but lacked the desire to fly for the airlines because the money just wasn't there.

It's not like it was worth it, anyway. With the recent economy of airlines and the high demand of younger pilots to replace the aging pilot population (in which the majority of pilots would reach the mandated 65 yrs. old age retirement set forth by the Federal Aviation Administration), things weren't meant to be in his favor.

An uneasy look came over Jenny's face after meeting the gaze of the pilot inside the elevator.

"Good morning, Jim," Wanda said, greeting the tired first officer, immune to Jenny's hesitation.

Jim nodded and returned the early morning greetings before he turned his attention casually back towards Jenny.

Jenny smiled at Jim as the three spread out inside the elevator, with her standing in the right rear corner of the steel box.

Jim paid close attention to Jenny as she fixed her necklace and then fidgeted and re-fixed her hair, an obvious sign of unease and nervousness.

"You okay?" Jim asked Jenny, finally breaking the awkward silence inside the elevator as it stopped at the next floor down.

"Fine," Jenny replied, cautiously glancing over to Wanda, who had been eyeing the uncomfortable interaction between Jenny and Jim.

The whole elevator ride was awkward for Jenny. She held a deep, dark secret which she vowed to never acknowledge, despite lingering text messages that served as distracting nuisances.

Jim and Jenny were staffed as crew together on a prior trip a couple weeks ago. Just after that trip in particular, Jenny had changed significantly. She became more isolated and not as exciting or adventurous.

Mitch had noticed and brought this up in conversation several times, but she had insisted that everything was fine, and that she just wanted to spend more time with her love.

The three smiled at one another as the elevator door closed once again. Jenny's heart pumped faster and an overwhelming feeling of claustrophobia set in the semi-full elevator. Or maybe it was the nerves in her stomach regarding the man who stood right beside her? She tried her best to ignore the angst, her stomach tightening uncomfortably from encountering Jim.

"Suppose we will meet the captain in the lobby before we catch the shuttle?" Jim asked rhetorically.

Jim was extremely new to the airline. He had passed his check ride a couple weeks prior and just got out of the simulators a month prior to that. He was as green as one could be for their first airline gig, without much experience.

Jim spent much of his time on duty talking about how his daughter was busy with gymnastics and dance class, and how his wife started to make a name for herself online as a pastry chef. He was as much of a proud family man as anyone who had everything they needed.

But there was something noticeably different about his approach to a conversation, especially when talking with cute females.

Jim, Wanda, and Jenny waited at a small café table for their captain to arrive. It wasn't like Mitch to be late. Capitalizing on his tardiness, Jim and Wanda ordered a small breakfast wrap and a coffee.

Shortly after reaching the lobby, Mitch emerged from the elevator, looking just as tired as Jenny and Wanda. Even Jim took notice of the fatigued look that came from his captain.

Before long, the airport shuttle was loaded up and ready to head out, full of business travelers and some weekend getaway-ers ready to board a cheap flight to wherever their destination was.

Chapter 1
Gate D9, LaGuardia Airport
06:45 a.m.

During the short ride into the terminal, the four crew members were among 15 passengers onboard the bus.

Most passengers on the bus struggled to wake up and thus had their aid of choice. Many elected to consume cups of coffee, which gave the bus a distinct New York coffee shop aroma.

There was a slight mutter of conversations seemingly drowning out the sounds of the bus driving over roads that had seen better days.

Jim tried to engage Mitch in some sort of conversation. Mitch had been giving Jim short-tempered and snarky responses the entire morning. It had been Mitch's passive-aggressive way of dealing with his pain and anger from the text messages that were found on Jenny's second phone when she was in the shower.

At one point, Jim's chin rested on the meaty portion of his hand, which was supported by his luggage. His face was one of unease, especially uneasy, yet visible nervous tick of scraping his finger nail along a scar under his chin from a bicycle accident when he was a child. He wasn't sure what had gotten into Mitch.

Mitch glanced down, stewing over the fact that he was waiting for the right moment to pop the question, even though that was now out of the cards.

The two flight attendants weren't paying much attention as they were off in their own world. However, Jim was caught off guard by Mitch's snarky responses, given the positive high marks from the previous two days of the four-day trip.

Jim thought that something was up with Mitch, and at one point, questioned if he was even fit to fly.

The early morning sun blasted through the eastern-facing window panes of the terminal. It overlooked the busy highway and the Citi Bank Stadium, where baseball lovers enjoyed a Mets game. On the other side of the terminal, the East River and Flushing Bay looked as calm as the early morning dew. The sunlight and vantage point gave LaGuardia Airport a spectacular view of not only the East River, but of the skyscrapers of Manhattan from across the water.

Looking west, the sunlight was absorbed by dark grey clouds off in the distance. A low-pressure system was inching its way into the New York area, and behind it was lousy weather all the way into the Great Plains.

Given the forecasts, every pilot wanted to expedite their processes and get their passengers loaded so they could take off before the storms hit.

LaGuardia had a long history of significant delays on the account of poor weather. Along with this factor, it was also a heavily trafficked airport. This meant a long and challenging day for anyone traveling through one of New York's busiest airports.

Through the busy belly of one of New York's three busy airports offering commercial services across the nation, Mitch and Jim casually walked through the TSA counters, then up to the gate area.

The aroma of coffee and sizzling breakfast scattered throughout the terminal, mixing with the typical buzz and harmony that made up the sounds of an airport.

Everywhere Mitch and Jim looked, the two caught glances from children who had their eyes to the sky, aspiring to be pilots just like them someday. Equally impressed were the women who always enjoyed a sharp-looking man in an equally sharp uniform. The two pilots looked like the professional airline pilots that their company expected of each of them, and the standards they seemed to have embodied for their passengers.

Their uniforms were pressed neatly, their hats sparkling clean with the brass wings polished. Their white shirts were absent of any stains, and their shoes were polished to a mirror finish.

Overall, they looked like general officers of the military who were the example of being "squared away." They knew it and were prideful of this at the same time.

As Mitch approached the desk first, Jim was left standing, looking out the window. Mitch chose the desk with the gate agent plucking away at her noisy keyboard while intently staring at her computer screen. She didn't seem to be overly friendly, for it was a hassle to be bothered by a passenger, let alone the pilots of that same flight.

One thing about Mitch was that he loved to give grief to uninterested and self-important gate agents. As he approached, he had a fake, naïve smile strung across his face. No one really noticed (or could tell the difference) between Mitch's genuine and fake smiles. After all, this was a requirement for the job.

After Mitch finished with the gate agent, Jim finally looked Mitch square in the eyes.

"Something gotten into you?" Jim asked, finally trying to break the icy silence between the two of them.

Mitch was obviously unhappy about something, but Jim couldn't really figure it out or why.

"Oh, I don't know, is there?" Mitch replied in a somewhat crotchety tone, not really letting his true feelings bleed out like he wanted to. It took every ounce of effort to keep his bottled-up rage inside. After all, he had a job to do, which was to govern the flight so his passengers could safely get to their destination.

Jim's mouth opened up slightly, like he was going to engage in a civil conversation, trying to pry what had gotten into the captain, but his attention was redirected by another sight. Out of the corner of his eye, he saw two stunning flight attendants coming off the movable walkway, who were both giggling and smiling.

Jim couldn't control himself; he really had a hard time with cute girls all dolled up. He especially loved the flight attendants looking to play the part of America's flight attendants of yester years.

Jenny caught the eyes of both Mitch and Jim as she walked past. Something didn't feel quite right. Jim's eyes were warm and kind, while Mitch's were cold and business-like. She hadn't seen Mitch so serious since they first started dating and he was pissed at his captain for being a complete douchebag.

"Good morning, Captain!" Wanda said with a perky little voice and a large smile on her face.

Mitch rose his head, which had been buried deep in the flight's paperwork, glancing over to where the warm voice had come from.

"Good morning, Wanda," Mitch said in a smooth, even tone before he plugged his head back into the dot-matrix-printed paperwork.

The paperwork contained all the important information that the flight was built on, including weights, speeds, weather, and times en route. It was everything that the pilot needed to run the flight safely.

The two flight attendants looked at one another, confused at the extremely odd and out of character interaction. Normally, Mitch was more of an outgoing guy, except when he wasn't. His attitude was very puzzling with the team as a whole. He was completely out of character for what he had been even just a couple hours prior.

Jenny leaned over towards Wanda and whispered, "He was fine earlier," referring to Mitch.

Wanda glanced over to Jenny and clarified, "Prince Charming?"

Jenny, caught off guard by the question, found herself fantasizing about her handsome captain before Mitch's voice brought her back to reality.

The buzzing activity within the gate area, along with the low rumble of conversations, added to the authenticity of a very busy airport. The passengers waited patiently for the jet's crews to get their morning started so they could have an on-time departure, which was a rarity at LaGuardia.

Mitch glanced around at many of the eyes that were on him and the rest of the crew from the passengers.

"Let's get onboard the jet and we'll do the brief quickly," Mitch said, going through the normal verbiage and focusing on his professional duties.

The Airlines' Flight Operations Manual specifically stated which briefings were required and even *when* they were required. A flight attendant brief was one of those briefs. Mitch couldn't wait to get through them and just get the day going, as most flight attendants rarely listened to what the pilots had to say. After all, most were just glued to their phones, texting their significant other, barely paying any attention.

Mitch turned and walked over to the gate's counter again. He unfolded the long-linked paperwork to a pre-determined spot and ripped the release into two sections. They were duplicates of the same information and the captain needed to sign the line above his name, as did the first officer, to acknowledge that the flight's paperwork was in order.

Mitch looked at Jim, and said, "I think this release is good to go. I think we are legal and accurate…What do you think, Jim?"

He was quizzing the new first officer to see if he could catch any mistakes that were presented in the long-linked paperwork.

A couple nearby passengers, a mother and a young daughter, overheard the captain quizzing the new first officer. Their ears perked up at some of the questions asked.

Another few passengers listened to the same questions as the mother and daughter exchanged an uneasy look. There was an unspoken feeling of anxiety between them regarding the qualifications of the crew.

Jim picked up the release and glanced over the entire release before starting at the top and going through each line of text.

"Well, if I was a company man, I'd say the release looks good, except for two things," Jim said, smiling nervously.

"Oh, and what is that?" Mitch shot back with his eyebrows raised.

"Well, for starters," Jim paused, "this release is for a CRJ-700, and if I were to look out the window, we're in a -900 today," Jim replied.

"Okay, good catch. What else?" Mitch asked, pushing the first officer to really hone his skills as a new airline pilot.

Jim looked at the release again. "We need a second alternate," pointing at the area on the release which identified the alternate airports, if planned.

"How do you see that?" Mitch asked, his eyes perking up, surprised at the good base level of knowledge that Jim had.

"Well, for the weather, we are looking at the one hour before and one hour after our ETA. We need greater than 2,000-foot ceilings and greater than three statute mile visibility. We don't have that. In fact, I looked at the weather this morning, and we'll have lower than minimums for most of the flight the further west we go. And if that's not enough, if we look at our first alternate and derive our minimums, we then need a second alternate."

"Nice job," Mitch complimented Jim. "Call up operations and have them cut a new release for us," Mitch said. "I'm going to get the Captain and the Pilot Flying preflight checks done, since I'll be flying this leg. I'll meet you on the jet shortly."

The gate agent took the signed release and looked it over for the two signatures, which were required to complete her tasks. Satisfied that everything was correct, she took the paperwork and folded it to the front page, which had all the crew members' names on top and began initialing her name next to each crew member's name on the release.

"Captain," the gate agent said.

"Yes, Ma'am?" Mitch replied.

"You're good to go," the gate agent said, while looking over Mitch's ID a second time.

"Thanks," Mitch nodded as he walked down the gate's jet-bridge connected to the aircraft.

The three other members of the crew lined up at the door leading to the jet-bridge with their identification badges prominently displayed, allowing for easy access for the gate agent to validate credentials against the release before allowing the rest of the crew onto the jet bridge.

The four boarded the de-powered jet, led by the Captain. Jim, trying to develop his own flow, decided to take Mitch's advice on how to accomplish the procedures to start the jet from what was called a "cold and dark cockpit," meaning the aircraft didn't have any electricity turned on. In this case, the aircraft would be dark, but Jim, being the prepared first officer that he wanted everyone to believe, brought a pen flashlight which he used to complete his checks before establishing power on the jet.

"Continue with your pre-flight procedures and I'll brief the flight attendants. We'll have customers come onboard in about ten minutes," Mitch said to Jim, implying an expedited inspection.

Mitch sat down in one of the first-class seats with Jenny and Wanda hovering over while the Captain went through his normal flight attendant briefing.

"Okay, just to let everyone know, we have a high-risk prisoner onboard with us this morning. Shouldn't be a problem since the gate agent also slipped a note within the release, telling us that we might have a Federal Air Marshal onboard," Mitch said. "We are looking at about a two-and-a-half-hour flight and fair weather for the most part. Lots of lower clouds and a storm to the west. There is potential for some more bumps over Tennessee, but overall, it looks mostly comfortable."

"Who is the prisoner?" Wanda asked uneasily.

"Well, I'm glad you asked…" Mitch said with a subtle smile. "His name is James Loecher."

"James Loecher?" Jenny asked, not really connecting the dots.

"Yes, James Loecher, the man who killed his lover and his lover's side-fling," Mitch said, staring sharply at Jenny, allowing his words to sink in with her.

Jenny's eyes grew large, but she remained speechless and glanced over to Wanda with a sign of discomfort.

Wanda glanced over at Jenny regarding the dark stare, along with Mitch's seemingly underlying tone of contempt.

Mitch got up and went into the flight deck to finish his pre-flight procedures just as the lights in the entire jet flickered. The power source transferred from the batteries to the jet bridge.

Jenny shrugged off Mitch's cold stare.

A few moments later, a clanking sound of chains and the sound of shuffling feet were heard coming down the long hallway leading to the aircraft.

A man emerged, chains clasped around his wrists and ankles, but in a tieless suit versus an orange jumpsuit, as movies portrayed. The two men escorting the man wore business casual attire, in what looked like cheaply produced blue rain jackets with yellow lettering on the back.

On board Nor'easter Flight 1172
06:55 a.m.

"Good morning, Captain," a shorter, thin-framed man said. He was wearing a blue jacket with the letters "FBI" labeled on the back.

Mitch reached around and shook the hands of the FBI agents.

"Please call me Mitch. I'm the captain for today's flight."

"Mitch, I'm Special Agent Mike Burkhart from the Bureau, and this is Richard Kennedy. We are going to take over the three seats right in front of the aft lavatory, I think seats 20 A, B, and C, unless you have any objections," Mike said with a slight smile.

"No, none at all," Mitch smiled greeted the FBI agents. "Just as always, please make sure he's seated next to the window and it should be a smooth flight for much of the trip," Mitch said calmly, glancing over at James Loecher, who was in regular clothes, but shackled.

"Captain," Jenny called out, "I'm going to grab a round of coffees for the four of us. What would you and Jim like?"

Mitch, with his back to Jenny, rolled his eyes before turning around and replying, "Black, and for Jim, nothing. He can suffer," Mitch mumbled to Jenny.

Jenny looked at Mitch oddly.

"Oh, okay. Two blacks it is," she replied softly. She looked at Mitch as if she wasn't really understanding the conflict that was brewing within him, but she had an unsettling feeling that Mitch knew something that he wasn't talking to her about.

And she had a slight inkling as to what it was.

As Jenny was getting ready to step off the aircraft, she had seen an opportunity to address the unnerving feeling she was getting from Mitch. Understanding the risk involved, she grabbed Mitch by his short-sleeved shirt and pulled him into the forward galley.

Mitch shot back, protesting angrily to getting pulled by his pristine shirt. "Hey, what are you doing, Jenny?!"

"What in the Hell is going on with you, Mitch? You've not been right all morning," Jenny snapped pointedly. "You've been very snarky and cold this entire morning."

Mitch looked at Jenny sideways. He reached to her butt, feeling the pocket where her phone had been securely held by the elastic in her pants.

Wanda looked down the aisle at the tense conversation between Mitch and Jenny, extremely thankful she wasn't in the middle of that issue. She shrugged her shoulders and continued with her pre-flight setup, ensuring that everything was good to go before they brought passengers on board.

Mitch looked at Jenny softly and calmly as he demanded, "Your phone."

Jenny's eyes grew huge. Feelings of being offended and violated had overridden any sort of love and playfulness that she usually exhibited. Carefully and slowly, she reached her rear pocket and pulled the phone out, placing it in Mitch's open hand.

Mitch looked at the phone and handed it back to her. "Not that one, your other one. The one that fell behind our bags in the hotel."

Jenny's innocent face quickly turned sour as she reached to her purse and pulled out her other phone, its backlight illuminating the screen that still showed unread messages.

"Unlock it," Mitch commanded, not taking into account what Jenny was feeling or thinking.

Jenny's fingers trembled slightly with fear and anger as she plucked away at her pin code.

"Jim's messages," Mitch said after Jenny unlocked the phone and handed it to him.

"You were going through my phone?" Jenny asked, trying to hide her pain, playing it off as being offended and surprised.

"Not hard to do when you set it next to my bag with it buzzing, facing up, so the whole world could read it," Mitch said softly.

Jenny's eyes started filling with tears as Mitch grabbed a napkin and handed it to Jenny.

"Only if you knew the truth, Mitch," Jenny whispered in a somber and semi-audible tone, secretly hoping that Mitch overheard.

"We'll talk about this later," Mitch said as he turned to see the first couple passengers entering the cabin through the jet bridge.

Jenny excused herself and quickly walked up the jet way into the terminal but stopped momentarily, glancing back towards Mitch. The passengers were already lined up and waiting eagerly to go. It was not common for an on-time departure from LaGuardia, so the passengers didn't want to jinx the experience.

Mitch sat back down into the captain's seat, sitting on the left side of the aircraft. Fixating on the middle post that divided the left and right windshields, he readjusted the sheep fur-covered seat for maximum comfort and proper visibility.

"We have our pre-departure clearance, you ready to go through it?" Jim asked, trying to show Mitch that he was at the top of his game.

"Before we go," Mitch said quietly, but with as much authority as an angry judge, "I'm not happy with you. I know. Now, let's get this trip over with, and we'll talk later about it."

Jim looked over at Mitch stunned. The knot in his gut was tight, along with his desire to get out of the awkward situation.

Mitch cleared his throat. "Okay, the Pre-Departure Clearance please."

"Oh, okay, the PDC…" Jim read through the whole clearance and validated much of the information, and then proceeded to plug in the validated information into the flight management computer. As Jim plugged the departure information in, he stopped halfway through and looked up. Mitch was entering the planned route into his iPad, building his departure sequence, making sure that he didn't miss any steps.

The flight, for the most part, was pretty routine for Mitch. He had flown that route numerous times, but he did need to have his head in the game for this flight in particular. A new first officer would require special attention, which meant an increase in workload considering Jim's lack of experience flying New York.

"Jenny?" Jim asked softly.

Mitch's ears perked up and he turned, looking at Jim square in his face as he sarcastically asked, "Who?"

Mitch turned around, got out of his seat, and exited the flight deck, skirting past the boarding passengers and into the forward lavatory.

Chapter 2
Gate D9, LaGuardia Airport
07:15 a.m.
Onboard Nor'easter Flight 1172

Mitch stepped out of the forward lavatory after a couple minutes of collecting himself. He stood in the entryway of the jet, his hat dazzling with its gold trim. He spent a couple moments looking at all the passengers, almost as if he was studying them, when he grabbed the intercom hand piece and put it up to his mouth.

"Ah, good morning," Mitch began, clearing his throat. "Ladies and gentlemen, I'm Mitch Bordoux, your captain for today's flight. We are very happy and excited to have you onboard today. We are going to get on our way here shortly. We are expecting a semi on-time departure this morning from LaGuardia, which, if you haven't experienced this airport before, is extremely rare," Mitch chuckled.

"Now, if you're not going to St. Louis, then you might want to check your boarding pass and make sure you're on the right airplane," Mitch joked with a smile. "Now, as we prepare the jet for departure, please pay attention to the flight attendants: Wanda in the back, and Jenny up front here, as they go through the safety briefings for this flight."

Mitch nodded at the passengers as he put the handheld microphone back in its cradle and re-entered the flight deck again, closing and latching the flight deck door behind him, allowing his expressionless face to set the mood for the flight.

"Okay, let's test your systems knowledge," Mitch said, interrupting Jim while watching him input data into the flight management computer.

"Oh, okay," Jim replied, not looking up from his task at hand.

"Where can we find the output for Pack 1?" Mitch asked, not allowing any time for Jim to fill the silent void.

Jim sat back for a moment and moved his hand over to the keys that paged through the synoptic pages of the jet's various systems, but before Jim could reply, Mitch barked another question.

"What happens if we have a reduced thrust temperature selected in the performance menu, and we turn on the anti-ice?" Mitch shot back with another question.

"Nothing," Jim responded instinctively.

"Wrong," Mitch replied sternly. "It reverts back to full thrust."

Flustered, Jim looked at Mitch and finally blurted out, "Mitch, what's gotten into you? What changed from yesterday and today?"

Mitch glared over at his new co-pilot as if shaming him for even calling out the captain.

Jim's shoulders slumped down, believing that he was caught red-handed for something. Not knowing what he was caught for was the worst.

"I-I think that you are upset with me," Jim remarked as he pointed towards the locked flight deck door. "Maybe I should not fly with you, we can get a ready-reserve pilot in 15 minutes."

Mitch glared at Jim and replied, "No, we are going to put our differences aside and have an on-time departure. You are not going to fuck this like you did with my girlfriend, so you're going to stay right there and do your job. In St. Louis, I don't care what you do."

Jim's eyes widened almost like they were going to pop out of his face. He sat in his seat speechless for a good, long couple of minutes. He rolled his wrist over, exposing his smartwatch face. It was 07:30- time to get rolling.

After a few administrative items were taken care of, Mitch looked over at Jim and said, "Call and get us a pushback clearance."

Jim nodded as he keyed up the microphone. A few moments later, the clearance to push back into the alleyway was obtained, and Mitch called out on the ground crews who had attached the tug and tow-bar to the nose-landing gear.

"Standby, firing up the APU," Mitch called over the interphone.

Mitch reached up and pushed a button on the overhead display, then looked at the secondary display for all of the proper indications.

Satisfied that the self-test was completed and all were performing normally, Mitch then selected the start switch, which started the smaller turbine-powered engine in the back of the plane.

The Auxiliary Power Unit (APU), was a strong enough powerplant to run the electrics all by itself, and if the conditions weren't too bad, the unit was able to run the pressurization and air conditioning as well.

Once the auxiliary power unit was running stably, Mitch gave the hand signal to one of the young ramp guys to disconnect the ground power.

"Okay, we are cleared to push, tail to the south, please," Mitch announced.

The flight deck had been roasting in the early morning sun. Everything was warm to the touch, including the black control columns.

In an effort to try and keep the cabin cool, Mitch elected to cool the cabin of the aircraft instead of giving everyone, including the flight deck, a bit of cool air.

With the pushback underway, Mitch reached up to the overhead panel and turned the mouth of a gasper vent, which pumped air into his face.

The forced air pushed the warm air through return vents and along the floor of the flight deck, taking with it the water vapor of Jim's coffee, which filled the flight deck with scents of a dark blended coffee..

A few seconds had elapsed as the jet had been pushed backwards.

Mitch could hear the faint sounds of the two flight attendants completing their required safety demonstrations through the door, as well as getting everything configured for the departure.

"Nor'easter Eleven Seventy-two, LaGuardia ground, we have a runway change for you. Instead of runway one-three, plan on runway four, the full length. Taxi to runway four via taxiway Alpha, Echo, and Bravo," the ground controller announced.

"Roger, we will plan on runway four via Alpha, Echo, and Bravo. Nor'easter Eleven Seventy-two," Jim relayed over the radio.

Mitch looked over at Jim, who had his hands in his lap and was looking out the window at the darkening clouds to the west.

"Run the numbers for the runway change. Four, full-length," Mitch said.

Mitch had the only side where the nose wheel steering was capable, so he brought up the thrust levers just high enough to get the jet rolling under its own power.

"Make sure your taxi and your takeoff checks are completed. We will be given an immediate takeoff clearance and if we aren't ready, we'll never have an on-time departure," Mitch said, warning Jim to stay ahead of the plane.

Jim nodded as he continued flipping switches and dialing knobs to configure the airplane for a smooth departure out of a highly-congested airspace.

Mitch rolled the jet onto the taxiway and looked over to Jim. "Okay, we're out of all the blind spots. You go ahead and put your head down and send for new numbers," Mitch said, keeping in line with division of labor principals.

The jet rolled softly through the various taxiway intersections as Mitch guided the jet through the assigned taxiways. Mitch was a seasoned pilot, but he was also a rule follower. When there were opportunities to cut corners, Mitch wouldn't, since it just wasn't in his nature. Everything needed to be cookie-cut precise and methodical.

Suddenly, an aural alert "Cell-Call," also known as SELCAL, blasted through the speakers.

"Fuck, the mechanics must have bumped the volume up on these new jets. See what the messages are," Mitch said.

"Okay, it's our new numbers. We are a full thrust, standing and bleeds will be closed. We'll leave the APU running for the departure," Jim said, dissecting the coded performance data.

"Got it," Mitch replied as he looked up to verify that neither one of the pilots had, in fact, shut down the auxiliary power unit.

"Nor'easter Eleven Seventy-two, LaGuardia tower, can you accept an immediate departure?" the controller asked.

Jim looked at Mitch, who was nodding affirmative. Jim keyed the mic, "Roger, Eleven Seventy-two, we are able immediate."

"Roger, Eleven Seventy-two," the controller said with a heavy New Yorker accent. "Line up and wait."

"Lining up and waiting, Nor'easter Eleven Seventy-two."

Mitch kept the power in as the jet rolled past the yellow-striped lines that indicated the line that aircraft should not cross unless authorized specifically by Air Traffic Control, known as the hold-short line.

"Nor'easter Eleven Seventy-two, you have traffic on a semi-long final to runway one-three, wind is zero-niner-zero at one-one. Runway four, you are cleared for immediate takeoff."

Mitch keyed up the microphone, "We have the traffic, runway four, cleared for takeoff. We're rolling, Nor'easter Eleven Seventy-two."

Jim quickly reached up and configured the landing and recognition light switches on the overhead panel, signifying that the aircraft was configured and cleared for takeoff.

The engines spooled up and Jim confirmed the stable acceleration on the engine gauges and looked over at the captain.

"Set thrust," Mitch commanded, releasing his hand from the thrust levers.

Jim instinctively grabbed the thrust levers, holding them in the position that the captain left them. He then checked the digital heading indicator and compared that to the runway they were taking off from.

"Thrust is set... and heading checks," Jim called out.

The jet's engines spooled up rather quickly in the warm, moist New York air, and the wheels began picking up speed as the pavement rushed beneath the aircraft.

"Eighty-knots," Jim called out about ten seconds after thrust application, being very disciplined in his duties as a first officer in his trained callouts.

Mitch looked down on his airspeed indicator as the speed tape rose steadily. "Checks," Mitch replied.

The lamp posts of the runway edge lights zipped past the side windows as the jet accelerated down the runway.

"V-one, and rotate," Jim announced as the jet accelerated past the pre-determined and pre-briefed speeds that allowed for a rejected take-off.

Mitch pulled the heavy controls back and let the nose of the jet gently lift off the ground. The white stripes of the center line on the runway disappeared from the windscreen and the jet's main wheels lifted off the ground as the jet majestically became airborne.

"Positive rate," Jim said firmly.

Mitch didn't immediately respond, and Jim looked over at Mitch to see why he was delaying the "gear up" call.

Satisfied with the altitude and speed, Mitch finally called out, "Gear up," after delaying his command a bit.

"Gear is coming up," Jim replied as he reached over to the forward center pedestal and grabbed the landing gear lever, bringing the lever to the up-and-stowed position.

The sounds of the hydraulics working to bring the gear up muffled throughout the cabin.

The jet climbed quickly: 100 feet, then 200 feet, until Mitch called out just below 400 feet, "Speed mode, and nav mode."

Jim nodded as his fingers moved through the selections on the autopilot panel, bringing the flight director's command bars up on the display, using them to guide the captain through the complex New York departure procedure.

"Nor'easter Eleven Seventy-two, contact departure," the controller broadcasted over the radio.

"Off to departure, Nor'easter Eleven Seventy-two, so long," Jim called back.

Jim was fiddling with the knobs that controlled the radio frequencies and their tuning when Mitch looked over at the task-saturated new first officer.

"So, how long have you been seeing Jenny?" Mitch blurted out, after holding it in for the past two hours.

Jim's fingers stopped cold, his face turning a deeply embarrassed red. He faced Mitch with his mouth open. He tried to say something, but before he could, Mitch gave another command.

"Flaps eight," Mitch called out.

A stunned Jim nodded and moved his hands to the left, where the flaps lever was located, and he moved the flaps from the 20-degree position to the eight-degree position. The climb segment of the trip allowed the jet to get configured for the next phase of flight, the post climb.

Jim turned back over to Mitch, started to open his mouth, but Mitch beat him to the punch. "Did you know she was also seeing someone else?" Mitch asked, growing agitated.

Again, Jim looked over at Mitch stunned. He started blubbering as he began trying to make a coherent sentence before Mitch interrupted once again.

"APU off and autopilot on," Mitch commanded, once again not allowing Jim opportunity to reply.

Jim reached across the panel and engaged the autopilot switch and the jet finally took over flying the complex procedure leaving the New York airspace. He then turned off the APU as the jet climbed through the first set of pre-assigned altitudes.

"Bring the flaps up and set climb thrust," Mitch announced as the jet's autopilot commanded a left turn, bringing the jet over the Hunts Point and Sound View in the borough of Bronx, bringing into view the Hudson River, Central Park, and the famous Yankee Stadium.

Within the first couple minutes in flight, the jet was climbing out of LaGuardia airspace, pointed out on a northern heading. The flight path would take the jet over the Hudson River, where Sully made his famous water landing, and then the route would point them west.

"Look, Mitch..." Jim began, but was cut off again, this time from the radio coming to life.

"Nor'easter Eleven Seventy-two, Departure, we had your transponder, but then it had cutout. Please recycle," the departure controller transmitted.

Mitch and Jim looked at the displays and the buttons on the main panel for any indications of false or failing components.

"Eleven Seventy-seven, we confirm we lost Transponder One. We'll recycle and get back with you," Jim called back on the radio.

"We have an ADS-B Out FAIL message on the EICAS," Jim called out, pointing at an illuminated light on the upper pedestal.

"Confirm, ADS-B Out FAIL, go into the QRH and look it up," Mitch demanded as he was flying.

Jim reached down to the cubby where his flight bag had been sitting. He fished around until he found a booklet that was the size of the Bible. He pulled out the spiral-bound book and started flipping through the pages so he could mitigate the issues.

Chapter 3
Inflight aboard Nor'easter Flight 1172
Somewhere over Pennsylvania
08:00 a.m.

During the climb-out, the dark grey clouds enveloped the jet in a subtle milky white as the sun's light dispersed among the droplets that made up the cloud. Turbulence rocked the jet a few times as Mitch climbed above the low level disturbance, giving the plane a well-needed bath after flying several days in a sandy environment.

After a short period of time, the jet leveled off at its cruising flight level, six miles above the earth, approximately 20 minutes after lifting off from LaGuardia.

The flight deck was silent, with no conversations and not even much in terms of radio traffic. The only sound was the occasional SELCAL alert, telling the crew that a new message arrived via their text messaging system from their dispatchers.

Looking out of the window, the clouds were building from the heat of the summer morning and the occasional rain showers that the jet flew through gave the jet a well-needed bath.

Mitch listened to the air hugging the frame as the jet accelerated to Mach 0.78. He focused on his captain tasks of checking in and completing a fuel check every so often, usually every 30 minutes, then reporting it to their dispatcher, advising of any trends.

Jim sat in his seat, monitoring the progress of the flight and watching for storms building to the left and the right of the jet.

Jim exhaled and looked over to Mitch. "Well, this is pretty awkward," Jim said hesitantly, hoping to break the icy silence between the two pilots in the flight deck after the revelation came out and both pilots knew a deep, dark secret.

The silence was a strain on Jim to begin with. It was exactly what his mother used to do to him when he was in trouble, and it drove him absolutely crazy.

Mitch looked over at the newly-minted first officer for a long minute, looking somewhat disturbed.

"You haven't been a pilot for the airline for more than a couple weeks, and yet you've already banged your first flight attendant!" Mitch snapped at Jim. "You should be proud! Aren't you married, by the way?" Mitch asked, glancing at Jim's wedding ring, hoping his words would pierce his soul like a butter knife through hot butter.

Jim let out another audible exhale. "I didn't know she was seeing you, Mitch. It just happened," he said hesitantly.

"Seeing me?" Mitch shouted. "Hell, I have the fucking engagement ring right here, in my flight bag! It was supposed to be HERS, tonight, on our last overnight before heading home!" Mitch scolded, leaving out the fact that Jenny had a second phone that he had no idea about until that morning.

Jim, feeling shammed by the whole situation, continued to look forward and stared at his multi-function display. He pretended not to be satisfied with the format, the image, and the range the map was showing. Trying to avoid further conversation, he reached to the right side of the panel, a somewhat angled panel housing multiple knobs, which controlled some of the various displays in front of him. He eyeballed the range knob, reached over, pinched, and then rotated the knob click by click to get a better view of the route.

The air vent blowing the air around the two men in the flight deck of the cramped CRJ-900 was probably the only thing that kept the two pilots from killing one another.

Mitch adjusted his face to get a blast of cold air and cool his enraged blood, which had been boiling up since he saw Jim earlier that morning.

Jim and Mitch sat silently, both in their own worlds. They were completing their procedural duties until a subtle knock on the flight deck door startled them.

Mitch glanced over to Jim as he attempted to reach around the seat to unlock the deadbolt, failing at first. He then twisted the buckle for the harness, freeing him from the five-point harness, which was a safety regulation to keep buckled while at a crew position, allowing him easier access to the door.

Behind the flight deck door, Jenny and Wanda prepared the galley for their services, which consisted of a small snack and enough coffee to satisfy a small army because of the early morning flight.

"Have you heard of James Loecher before?" Jenny asked, looking at Wanda.

"Rumor had it that he found his wife cheating on him and claimed that their kid wasn't his, so he proceeded to kill both of them," Wanda said. "And apparently it wasn't the first time this happened, since he was wanted in Missouri for something similar. He's mental."

"Sounds like it," Jenny replied.

"That's not all," Wanda continued. "Apparently while he was being held at Rikers Island, he went batshit crazy. He was stone-cold one moment, and highly violent the next. Something's not right upstairs."

"Growing up," Jenny said, "we had a guy on our block who was violent and Schizophrenic. I think the doctors said he had aggression and impulsivity-based Schizophrenia. It scared the shit out of me because he was, like you said, fine one moment, then the next, he was crazy."

Wanda shrugged her shoulders, knowing full well that neither of them were doctors, so they didn't really know what was going on inside James' mind. They just knew he was high-risk.

"Off to the captain," Jenny said uneasily after topping off two cups, making her way silently to the flight deck. The way she moved was almost as if someone was completing the walk of shame after a wild party night.

She sat the two cups of black coffee down to both of the pilots as a means of starting a conversation, almost like a peace offering. She looked like she had been kicked in the proverbial stomach.

Mitch didn't care to initially say a word, but finally broke the silence with, "What is it, Jenny?" in a monotone, all-business, no-nonsense voice.

Jenny felt like she had overstayed her welcome, but still stood her ground. She turned around, closed the door and locked it, making sure it was just the three of them.

Jenny cleared her throat and looked at Jim.

Jim turned ghostly white as Jenny looked back at Mitch, and began, "I don't even know what to say…"

"Thank you, Jenny. That'll be all," Mitch said, interrupting Jenny mid-sentence, in an attempt to shut off a serious conversation. Mitch's stern tone of voice was something that haunted Jenny every time he used it, which was so infrequent. She prayed that it was never used against her, but it finally was in this moment, and it was downright destructive inside.

Mitch used that tone a couple of times when he was dissatisfied or downright angry. Unfortunately for him, he was easy to read, as he wore his feelings on his sleeve, especially for Jenny.

She straightened her shirt and scarf, turned around, and left the flight deck. Jim followed behind closely to ensure that the flight deck door was latched and that the locking bar was engaged.

Jenny heard the door's latching mechanism engage, and with the door securely shut and locked, she leaned back on the door and dropped her head. She grabbed the hair sticks that held her hair in place and pulled them out, allowing her long brown hair to fall and drape over her face.

For Jenny, the act of hiding her face was something she did ever since she was a child when she felt like she had done wrong and was then scolded by her father. It was a ritual for her, as she always seemed to get into trouble often, especially in school and for hanging out with the boys.

With subtle tears rolling down her cheeks, Jenny's knot-tight stomach began aching. The feeling of loving one, and then cheating on him, if you could really call it that, wasn't something she had planned on. It was once, after a few beers.

"Surely the courts would go in my favor, if I ever decided to press charges," Jenny said to herself. She shook the thought out of her head, as she knew that her father was right.

She invited such actions just because of how she dressed and how much of a flirt she was. Who would believe her? Moreover, what would happen to her career if she claimed that she was the victim of something traumatic? How would people treat her differently, if at all?

Suddenly, Jenny found herself scratching the inside of her forearms and wrists, the scars and memories of previous self-mutilation ever present.

Squeezing her eyes, Jenny found herself flashing back to her time at Camp Pendleton, when she was enlisted in the Marine Corps. She had just gotten back from an 11-month deployment to Afghanistan where she was based, holding down a Forward Operating Base (FOB) in the mountains, northeast of the country.

The nights were spent in an over-watch tower, looking over the mountainous terrain to the west with another marine, Simpson, one who looked like a life-sized version of the GI Joe figurine.

Most nights were quiet, as the Taliban didn't have as many nighttime operation capabilities available. It was basically a tour of just sitting and relaxing in an air-conditioned office 50 feet in the air with windows on all four sides, looking out over the mountains, not too far off in the distance.

One night, as it was getting towards the end of the fighting season, usually around the first snowfall in the mountains, Jenny found herself gazing through the advanced night vision goggles. It didn't have the range of normal binoculars, but it could pick up light like a bright beacon from miles away.

While scanning the mountains on a particular night, a bright flash caught Jenny's eye. It was faint, but it was definitely a light-emitting source.

Jenny reached over to her radio and keyed up the microphone. Once it became live, a muzzle flash caught her from the corner of her eye, followed by a snap and buzzing sound as an AK-47 round ricocheted off the bulletproof glass.

Jenny's heart stopped for a split second while she attempted to regain her bearings.

Just as she acquired the target, a lone gunman hiding behind two large rocks about 500 meters away, a distinct sound of a rocket motor perked her ears.

However, the sound only lasted for a second. It sounded like a quick clap of thunder.

Before she knew it, the base of the tower took a direct hit from the rocket.

Losing its ability to stand, the tower toppled over under its own weight. The feeling of momentary weightlessness was followed by a falling sensation as the cab of the tower fell 50 feet, crashing on its side into the Container Housing Units, which were metal shipping containers set up as living quarters, right beneath it. The loud crash had awoken half the base.

In the sheer chaos of the attack, which only lasted about 30 seconds, Jenny lost sight of Simpson, her colleague. He was on the side of the tower that hit the ground first.

It wasn't too long before the Calvary of emergency responders arrived to render aid and search through the rubble. Jenny was pulled out without much of an injury because she had kept her protective equipment on during her shift. She was better than she physically looked and only suffered a couple cuts and bruises.

She soon found herself in the ambulance, getting moved over to the medical facility. She later found out that Simpson, who regularly did not wear any protective gear, wasn't so lucky. They found his body among the remains of six other service members when the tower crashed into the building as the occupants slept.

The slight bumps of turbulence, along with an "Excuse me, stewardess," male in seat 2D shocked Jenny back to the present.

Without wasting a second, Jenny ducked inside the galley, right next to the Galley Service Door, for a quick moment to reset her hair and clean up her mascara, which had been a mess after her cold, heartless encounter with the captain. Once she righted herself, she put her mind to taking care of her first-class passengers, trying to bring some sort of resemblance of normalcy to her operation. After all, she was the lead flight attendant.

One of the other passengers sitting in the aisle seat of 5B was quietly observing Jenny, and her somewhat obvious emotional challenges.

While observing, the man noticed on her lanyard, a somewhat worn emblem that was affixed next to her company ID, it was an eagle, a globe and an anchor, commonly referred to as the Marine Corps Emblem.

The man noticed Jenny's thousand-yard stare, which was a common trait for those who had seen battle.

As Jenny walked by, she noticed that a particular pair of eyes were tracking her. It normally didn't bother her, but when she glanced over at the man's eyes, she had caught the same characteristics, the thousand-yard stair, that the man noticed on her.

There were some characteristics that veterans shared, especially after deploying to a war-zone. Those characteristics were relatively obvious when one veteran came face-to-face with another veteran, whereas the general public would overlook.

"Excuse me, miss, you okay?" the fellow veteran asked from seat 5B.

Jenny paused by the unexpected question, "Ah yeah, just trying to get my head screwed on straight for these early morning flights," Jenny replied with a fake but believable smile.

"I know a line of bullshit when I hear it," the man in the seat chuckled slightly.

Jenny gave the man an odd look, tilting her head like dogs do when they don't understand something.

The man looked up at Jenny, pointed at her emblem, "Don't worry, I won't ask you anything. I just wanted to introduce myself, I'm Bill," he said, extending out his hand, hoping to strike up a small conversation.

"Jenny," she replied, meeting Bill's outreached hand.

"Been a hard transition?" The man asked. "Trying to juggle life and keeping yourself from folding? Am I right?" Bill asked, pretty much hitting the nail on the head.

Jenny smiled at Bill, but the burst of emotion was about to burst like a cork in a champagne bottle. She excused herself quickly into the lavatory, where she sat on the toilet seat with tears streaming from her eyes uncontrollably.

After regaining some resemblance of composure, Jenny grabbed her cellphone, selected Mitch's text message and began typing and plucking away at the messaging services. Before long, Jenny had finished what seemed to look like an entire novel on her phone. She made sure that the Wi-Fi was showing as connected, selected "send," and verified that the "sent" receipt was present before she went back to her work.

Chapter 4
In flight, Nor'easter 1172
08:30 a.m.

"Nor'easter Eleven Seventy-two, turn right heading three-zero-zero, for weather," the center controller called out.

Jim replied as professionally as he could regarding the radio callouts. The turbulence hadn't been too bad to warrant turning on the seatbelt sign. A couple bumps here and there were what had been expected for the flight.

"Let's turn on the weather radar and paint some pictures," Mitch said. "What are some of the rules with the radar?"

"Don't stand within two feet of it while it's running?" Jim replied.

"Unless you don't want kids, which is highly recommended for you," Mitch jabbed, looking at any excuse to throw a verbal punch at his co-pilot. The efforts were futile.

Jim looked over at Mitch, once again, trying to break the ice. "When I was younger, I worked at a television studio. The dishes, uplink, and downlinks that were available, I used to roast hot dogs with the energy. It was like having a microwave without a box. Pretty cool stuff."

Mitch continued with his fuel check, completely unphased with the story. He carried on with his duties, picking up the new fuel calculations based on their current conditions.

"We should land with an extra four grand in the tanks," Mitch said.

"That's good to hear," Jim replied, not really knowing why Mitch decided to speak up.

Mitch sat up and glanced at the developing storms, thinking.

"For someone who slept with another guy's girlfriend, you sure aren't as apologetic as I would expect," Mitch finally voiced, one of the many questions and observations that he had.

Jim glanced over, trying to play it off. "What are you suggesting?" Jim asked.

"I'm not suggesting or insinuating anything, but normally when someone is working this close to the guy whose girlfriend you slept with, you're not exactly remorseful," Mitch retorted.

Jim snickered very slightly before responding. "What would make you feel better, Captain?" Jim asked sarcastically, motioning, and gesturing his open palms towards Mitch.

Mitch squinted slightly, taking in the visual cues that Jim exhibited, that were completely out of character for the man.

"I see," Mitch replied. His rage against Jim only festered even more inside of him.

Meanwhile in the cabin, on the backside of the locked flight deck door, Wanda had been finishing the last couple rows for drinks and other service items when an early teen, sitting alone in seat 19A, reached over and nervously whispered into Wanda's ear, "Is he dangerous?"

"Not anymore," Wanda said smiling, glancing at the man in the next seat back, before returning her attention back to the kid.

Wanda looked over at James again. He was silent, barely looking around. He seemed as if he was just mentally absent from the world, or mildly sedated so as to not cause any trouble.

Pushing the cart to the next row back, Wanda thought silently to herself, "I guess having six murders under your belt helps in the 'zero-fucks given' department."

As Wanda reached the last row, she asked if the guards needed any further drinks, but made sure she didn't interact with the prisoner, as was company policy. They didn't get any service for such a short flight.

As Wanda began pulling the galley cart back up the aisle, her eyes locked onto the eyes of the man sitting in seat 13B. Something was different about him from the other passengers. The difference was subtle, but there was definitely something amiss about him. He definitely had the vibe of an air marshal, but their assigned seats were empty when the flight left the gate.

James looked over at his guard, who sat next to him, monitoring his every movement.

Speaking his first words onboard, James grunted, "Can I use the toilet?" fairly submissive to his row mate.

"Do you really need to go?" Agent Richard Kennedy asked, annoyed that the question was even brought up for such a short flight.

James gestured, knowing full well that he couldn't control when his bodily functions needed to be attended to.

Kennedy sighed and looked over at Mike. "What do you think, Mike?"

"We have over an hour left, I'd like to use the restroom," James interrupted, double-downing on his request, making sure that he played off his innocents.

Mike Burkhart sat across the aisle from Richard, and he looked over at James as he took a deep breath, rolling his eyes.

"Okay, better make it quick."

"I hate this part," Mike said to Richard as he motioned over at James, who sat motionless, waiting to be released from his seat.

"Thank you," James sneered sarcastically.

Richard reached over to the lap belt that restrained James into the seat and flipped the release lever, freeing James to get up from his seat. The arm rest on this jet did not raise up, so it was a challenge from the very beginning to try and get someone who was already immobilized to navigate out of the seat without getting snagged on anything, let alone maneuver around a small airplane.

Richard got up into the aisle and stood straight up. He took a step towards the rear galley, at the tail of the plane, allowing James to get up and out of his seat. James took tiny side-steps until he stepped into the aisle way, which led to the rear lavatory. There had been no movement toward the back of the plane, so the lavatory remained unoccupied for the previous several minutes.

Most of the passengers in the last half of the plane didn't pay any attention to James' carefully orchestrated movements.

Just as he started moving towards the rear lav, about six feet away in distance, the jet entered a pocket of highly unstable air. The jet's nose dipped for a second, then bounced back up to a nose-high attitude. Everything in the cabin floated for a mere moment, until the jet's orientation changed once again.

With the nose of the jet pointing down again, everything that had levitated suddenly came crashing back down, hitting the floor hard. Sounds of crashing items overcame the moderately loud engine sounds.

The gasps and screams of the unexpected turbulence panicked passengers. Unsure of what was happening, several scared passengers looked around, catching the moment that James had white-knuckled the back of his seat, trying to keep his balance. Richard did the same thing.

Again, another dip of the nose, with a subsequent crashing to the floor. Richard floated somewhat as the jet entered a momentary zero-g drop. As Richard landed back on the floor, he lost his balance after stepping on the slack of James restraints, which were flying around with the turbulence.

The strong bumps occurred again, and the chains managed to get caught around Richard's leg, which caused James to fall backwards onto Richard.

James' elbow landed with full force onto Richard's chest, snapping a couple ribs.

Richard let out a large yelp as another large jolt of the airplane brought James airborne, pulling Richard's leg into an awkward position and causing an audible snap. Richard's leg had snapped right at the point where the chains cinched down.

Richard tried to catch his breath while James laid on top of him, attempting to get up. Mike managed to get out of his seat and began working to untangle the chain from Richard's foot without having to unsecure James' securement.

"Hang on!" Mike shouted to Richard.

The struggle intensified between the two men laying on top of one another in the aisle. James' jostling hid his actual hand movements, which gave unobstructed access to Richard's service weapon.

A few seconds of struggles passed when suddenly, a loud, percussive bang reverberated throughout the cabin, originating from the last row.

The percussive discharges of the gun caused everyone inside the jet to cover their ears from the intense burst of deafening noise.

Jenny, who was serving hot rolled-up towels in the first-class cabin, saw the movement out of the corner of her eye towards the back, but didn't pay much attention until the gunshots rang out.

The smell of spent gunpowder circulated throughout the aft portion of the cabin.

The cabin fell silent and passengers were horrified with the sudden realization that a gun had been fired onboard the aircraft.

Mike fell backwards in the aisle, between the seats, grasping his chest with his right hand. As he frantically tried reaching for his gun, he lost consciousness.

There was a collective gasp and cry.

Richard was still in a haze, trying to catch his breath. He still had the mental clarity to try and grab onto James' chains and give a last-ditch effort to somehow re-secure and regain some control over the situation as well as James.

Richard grabbed ahold of James' restraints and pulled his chains as tightly as he could, but James was quicker.

Jabbing Richard's stolen gun under his ribcage, James tightly grasped the guns grip and swiftly pulled the trigger. Another loud percussive bang shook the floor of the jet as Richard laid motionless under James.

"Oh my God! He's got a gun!" one of the passengers shouted. The rest of them were getting reoriented with their surroundings after the major turbulence, but it was clear that things had taken a turn for the worse onboard.

Wanda, who was working in the Galley, spun her head around galley wall, giving her a clear line of sight of the commotion in the back of the jet.

Just as the man in seat 18B called out the disruption, all eyes in the back half of the plane shot backwards towards James, who was still in the aisle, but was struggling with getting himself untangled and freed from his shackles.

The man sitting in the aisle seat of 19C saw a small opportunity, quickly got to his feet, and lunged towards James in an effort to gain control of the situation.

Out of the corner of his eye, James was quick to react. The man had barely stood up before James pointed the gun at his center of mass and pulled the trigger a couple times.

The gun barked each and every time, spitting out hot lead. The bullets found their mark as the man fell face-first on the floor, one of the bullets penetrating the man's shoulder and exiting out the rear, nicking the shoulder of a young mother who was sitting a couple rows ahead of him in row 15.

Jenny took Wanda by the hand and retreated into the galley. The two ducked down after the initial gunshot. Jenny covered Wanda with her body, holding her body against the service door of the jet, like a mother protecting her children from danger.

James quickly gauged the other passengers, who were crying and weeping for the good Samaritan.

Keeping an eye on the rest of the passengers, James rolled over and untangled the chains from Richard's broken leg and then retrieved the handcuff keys from Richard's pocket.

Getting to his feet, James freed himself from the metal shackles, allowing him to have free access to the aircraft without any sort of physical restraints.

Out of breath but full of adrenaline, James took a deep breath in and scanned the cabin once again, looking for any other potential hostiles.

Not believing his incredible luck, James glanced down at Richard, who laid motionless, blood saturating the carpet around where the gunshot wound was.

James got straight up and started walking towards the front of the jet before making eye contact with the kid who had inquired about him a short time ago.

"She lied," James chuckled, referring to Wanda answering the kid's question from earlier.

The kid curled up into his seat, his knees to his chest.

"Everyone, head and eyes FORWARD!" James commanded sternly.

Again, scanning the crowd, James shouted, "Don't try to be a hero like this guy. If I can see your eyes, you are wrong. Don't let me see your eyes."

Satisfied that the passengers mostly heeded this warning, James rolled Richard over and grabbed his extra two magazines. Then he went over to Mike and grabbed his firearm, along with his extra ammunition.

Passengers watched in horror as they realized they were the first successful hijacking since September 11th.

One man in particular was watching more intently than others. It was the man in seat 13B, who sat quietly, trying to blend into the environment that he was now a part of.

"Head and eyes forward!" James shouted.

Jenny got up from her covering position in the forward galley and grabbed ahold of the nearby beverage cart, which she used as cover. She gave the cart a giant push down the aisle, hoping that the cart would find its way down the backend of the airplane and immobilize the hijacker.

James turned around, watched the cart roll about halfway down the aisle and stop, without hitting anything. The aim was decent, but the momentum wasn't there. James was un-phased with the fruitless attempt to slow him down and continued making his way towards the flight deck.

Horrified that the cart hadn't done as intended, Jenny turned and ran into the forward jump seat. Her high heels dug sideways into the floor, twisting her ankle. Her ankle stung at the onset of the strain.

Fighting against the pain, Jenny's hands struggled to find a metal piece of the seat to grab onto.

Finally, a solid piece of the chair sat firmly in her hands and she yanked the seat from its stowed position, using the momentum to latch the seat into its heavy-duty locking receptacles. This kept access to the flight deck minimized. The company training was to protect the flight deck at all costs and slow the advancement of an attacker, but nothing else was readily available in terms of training that Jenny and Wanda had gone through.

As James continued moving slowly past the different rows of terrified passengers, his focus was lasered on the two flight attendants in the forward galley. While he moved forward, he occasionally glanced left and right, checking to make sure the passengers were following his instructions.

Trembling from the rush of adrenaline, Jenny fumbled with the interphone in an effort to grasp it. The interphone was located right next to the front entryway, but her fine motor skills were so deteriorated that it felt like she was operating with a set of rubber fingers. She couldn't find the dexterity to push the buttons she wanted to in order to call up the flight deck.

Finally, after what felt like ten minutes, Jenny's fingers finally overcame the spring-resistance and punched the EMER button on the phone's handset and chimed the flight deck.

Mitch answered extremely abrasively, "What the Hell is going on back there?!" yelling through his headset, which was tied into the intercom system.

"H-h-hijacker," Jenny yelled, trying to make her vocal cords work, overcoming the paralyzing fear as well as the excruciating pain of her ankle.

Mitch looked over to Jim, "Oh my God," Mitch replied, keying the transmit button, "is it our prisoner?"

The line had gone silent, but the handset was still active.

On the other side of the flight deck door, James approached Jenny with the muzzle of the gun trained at her forehead, he mouthed the words, "Put it down," and Jenny complied slowly.

Jenny's eyes fixated at the barrel of the gun, her blood pressure rising to the point where she began seeing stars in her eyes. The stars triggered a strong flashback to Afghanistan, when she watched in slow motion as the rocket motor ignited and the rocket blast that shot the rocks ten feet back from its powerful exhaust. Each rock was clearly visible in her night vision goggles, like a bright shooting star.

James snapped his fingers in front of Jenny's face before she jolted back to reality and the hijacking. She felt the eyes of the first-class passengers on her, a face full of terror from having a gun trained at her point-blank.

Jenny squeezed her eyes, trying to shake off the bout of PTSD and focus on the moment.

In the flight deck, Mitch and Jim looked at one another with deep concern, covering their faces as they listened to the live-line.

"Call ATC, and get us…" Mitch's voice fell silent when the male voice of the hijacker came on the line.

"Get you what? Captain?" James snarled through the handset.

"What do you want?" Mitch asked.

"Open the door," James demanded.

"No. I will not, try again." Mitch replied, overly defiant.

"Open the door, or this pretty flight attendant will be no more," James demanded once again, pressing the muzzle of the gun against Jenny's temple region, the black rings of the spent gun powder transferring to her skin.

"Kill every passenger back there, and I still won't open the door!" Mitch yelled defiantly again.

"Suit yourself," James laughed.

Sounds of screaming were heard as a commotion erupted in the cabin, filtering through the open microphone on the handset.

Mitch and Jim looked at one another. "At no point will we open the door. Remember that!" Mitch yelled sternly at Jim, looking him square in the eyes.

Jim's face turned a pale white as the blood drained from his face, when a deep male voice came back on the line along with James.

"Tell the captain your name."

Jim, who was already inputting data into the ACARS screen and the texting function, stopped typing and his head shot up and looked at Mitch. His palms were sweaty and his forehead had beads of sweat dripping down his cheek.

The male on the other line muttered, "Frank, F-Frank Weinhaus," the man said, stuttering, trying to form a coherent response.

"Hi Frank," James replied. "Please tell the captain if you have any children."

Frank's voice sounded crackly and choppy, as he got out, "I-I have two d-daughters." He was sobbing and his voice was weak and submissive.

"I have two daughters, they're good girls," Frank said again, crying out.

"Okay, so what is it that I want?" James asked, forcing the demand while holding Frank at gunpoint.

Mitch's hair stood on end at the back of his neck. His knot in his stomach from earlier this morning became even tighter.

"H-H-He wants you to l-let him into the cockpit," Frank replied, sounding stressed and submissive to James.

"I cannot do that," Mitch said sternly.

"Oh Jesus," Frank cried out, "he's got a gun to my head. Please, please do something!"

Suddenly, a loud pop was heard through the door followed by the sound of what could only be described as a bag of potatoes hitting the ground.

Frank collapsed to the floor.

The interphone came live again as James snickered, "Frank's blood is on your hands, Captain. Should we have another lesson in compliance? I want the door open."

Jim and Mitch looked at each other again, stunned at what they had just heard.

"No!" Mitch cried out.

"Suit yourself, if you're not going to open the door, then LAND THIS AIRPLANE!" James snarled and disconnected the intercom.

Mitch's head sank into his hands, almost like he was unwilling to face reality or that this was *actually* happening right now. He was never directly responsible for someone's death.

Suddenly, a repetitive loud bang echoed through the flight deck. The meaty part of a fist was pounding on the door.

Mitch and Jim both jumped in their seats, but then ignored the pounding, as per protocol.

Mitch looked back to verify that the door was indeed latched, finally yelling to Jim, "Get on the horn and radio this in!"

Jim reached over to the center pedestal and dialed in the international code for hijacking on the transponder.

He keyed up the microphone, unintentionally stepping on the other radio traffic that was going over the airways. "Mayday mayday mayday, Nor'easter Eleven Seventy-two, declaring an emergency."

It took a moment, but then Jim heard the squealing sound of the radio feedback that usually occurs when two radio transmissions are broadcasted at the same time.

"Previous aircraft calling, you were stepped on, please repeat," the controller called back.

The radio was silent, noting the hesitation from the controller until Jim keyed up the radio once again and said, "Center, Eleven Seventy-two, we are declaring an emergency!"

There was a long pause over the airways, but within 15 seconds, a different voice came over the network. "Nor'easter Eleven Seventy-two, understand your emergency, squawking seventy-five hundred. Standby one moment."

The back of Mitch's neck had goosebumps up and down it after the transmission finished.

"Eleven Seventy-two, Center, state your intentions." The controller called out.

Mitch looked at Jim, who was as pale as a ghostly figure before he keyed up the microphone, "We need to land. Give us suitable options for us." Mitch called out.

"Eleven Seventy-two, we have your request, lets switch you to another frequency and we will discuss further. Is the flight deck secure?" The controller asked.

"Eleven Seventy-two," Jim replied over the frequency, acknowledging that the aircrew heard and understood the transmission.

Jim looked over at Mitch, his heart pounding and his mind racing. In his mind, he was still a brand new first officer. No one and nothing had ever truly prepared him for this sort of event yet.

"Ah, Nor'easter Eleven Seventy-two, understand the nature of your emergency, contact Chicago center at one-three-two point one," the controller announced over the airways.

"Off to one-three-two point one, Eleven Seventy-two," Jim nervously called back to the controller.

Jim fumbled over tuning the radio. He twisted the tuning knob, but his hands were shaking so much that he kept on passing the frequency that he was looking for. He turned the dial one way and then passed the mark, then turned the dial the other way and passed it again. Then he would turn it back the first way, passing it yet again.

"Goddammit," Jim scolded himself, cursing at his inability to perform the simplest task.

Mitch reached over and put his hand on top of Jim's. "Let me tune it," Mitch said, trying to instill a calmness in the newly-minted first officer.

"Oh-okay," Jim replied, agreeing that Mitch could do a better job.

"Slow down. You're racing right now. You're nervous, but slow down and be deliberate," Mitch said, trying to calm Jim.

Mitch calmly tuned the radio and keyed it up on the discrete frequency, "Center, this is Eleven Seventy-two, with you."

"Eleven Seventy-two, roger, please state the nature of your situation."

Mitch calmly presented the facts over the radio, as much as he could remember. These transmissions were being recorded, and Mitch needed to ensure that he was providing only what he knew versus what he thought.

"I understand, give us a couple of minutes, we've got a lot of bad weather below you and to the south of you. Most airports are below minimums, so unless you absolutely need to, stay at altitude as long as you can while we get a plan of action going here," the controller said.

"Roger, standing by. We want to get down as soon as we can. We are about 90 minutes out of St. Louis, maybe that's our best bet?"

"We are suspecting the same thing, but keep in mind, you will be getting some company shortly. Also, the FBI will be brought into the conversation, too, together, we can figure out the perfect place to land." the controller said, hinting at the likelihood of a fighter jet escort.

Mitch keyed up the microphone again and said, "Two prisoner escorts were armed FBI special agents as well," without any idea that both the agents were now dead.

Mitch looked over at Jim, whose face was still pale white.

"Jim, stay with me. We're going to be okay," Mitch said calmly. "That door we are behind, per TSA standards, can take 9mm round. As long as we don't offer to open the door, we have control of the flight."

"B-but Frank…" Jim began, but was interrupted.

"Yes, remember Frank, but remember our job is to get this plane down as soon as possible so the other passengers have a chance to live," Mitch said with a huge pain in his voice.

Mitch looked down on the flight management computer, and he pulled up the aircraft text messaging system that linked the aircraft with their dispatcher.

"Confirm FAM onboard," Mitch typed out, remembering the Federal Air Marshal who was supposed to be onboard the jet… but wasn't.

Chapter 5
Flight 1172, In flight,
Somewhere over Columbus, Ohio
08:45 a.m.

"Nor'easter Eleven Seventy-two, slow to your long-range cruise," the center controller called out. "We have some company getting organized and we're still trying to figure out a landing spot for you."

"St. Louis is our best bet right now, we think," Mitch announced over the radio, acknowledging that a lot could happen in the next hour.

"Okay, sounds good, let's plan on that. It'll give the FBI some time to set up shop out there. Has he made any demands?" the controller replied.

"Just to land." Mitch replied, "and, understood about our long-range cruise, give us a couple minutes, we'll need to do some math up here," Mitch called back to the controller.

Jim turned his company-issued iPad on, his fingers bouncing around at the more moderately intense turbulence. The iPad contained all the manuals and charts for the aircraft. After paging through a few different publications, Jim brought up the performance charts for maximum endurance. Cross-referencing the weight of the jet with their altitude of 34,000 feet and their weight, Jim was able to come up with their most economical cruise numbers.

"Okay, we are looking at Mach 0.725 at our current weight and altitude," Jim announced as Mitch pulled the power back and reset the speed bug.

Mitch and Jim sat quietly in the flight deck, both deep in thought. The voice of the innocent passenger who was just murdered due to their inaction was replaying over and over again like a persistent nightmare in their heads.

"Bordoux, let us take it from here."

Mitch's mind flashed back to a previous traumatic experience, except the first responder's voice was Frank's.

Mitch's attention shot back to the present with the sound of a radio call blurting through the headset.

"Center, Dagger One-one, a flight of two, checking in," the radio called out. The pilot's voice sounded calm and cool over the radio.

Mitch always wanted to be a fighter pilot. He was told that was the best way to enlist, then cross-train into a pilot slot.

"Dagger?" Mitch said to a listening ear, with a puzzled look on his face.

Jim looked over and asked, "What's that?"

Mitch glanced over at Jim, saying, "Dagger, that's a fighter call sign."

"Dagger Flight, target aircraft is a hijacker Canadair Regional Jet, 12 o'clock about 15 miles," the controller said, guiding the pilots to the hijacked target aircraft.

"Dagger One-one copies, joining up, we have radar contact on the target."

Two seconds passed with silence over the radio when the controller finally chimed in, "Nor'easter Eleven Seventy-two, you have two fighters coming up from the Ohio fighter squadron, they'll be your escort."

Mitch quickly shook his head, making Jim do a double-take.

"What's going on, Mitch?" Jim asked.

Mitch looked over at Jim with a little bit of a grin on his face. Finally, he thought, something was moving in his favor today.

"What?" Jim asked again, not understanding the meaning of the last radio transmission or the smile on Mitch's face.

"That's my fighter unit," Mitch replied.

"Your fighter unit?" Jim asked, not understanding the connection.

"Yeah, I'm attached to the Ohio Air National Guard, an F-16 fighter base. I guess that you didn't realize we were right over their base," Mitch explained.

"Oh, I didn't know you were military," Jim replied, still not making the connection.

Mitch read Jim's face again. "You don't get it. These jets, I know many of the pilots personally. When they deploy for their rotations overseas, I fly with them when they travel. I move their equipment."

Somewhat annoyed that Jim wasn't getting why he was somewhat excited, Mitch keyed the microphone, "Center, Eleven Seventy-two, confirm the two jets are from the one-twelfth?"

"Nor'easter Flight, this is Dagger One-One, joining on your left wing, and yes, we are from the one-twelfth. We were on a training mission and heard you needed some help. So, we gassed up and headed your way," the lead fighter pilot replied.

An audible "thank God" was heard over the radio.

The jets settled in formation with the hijacked airliner. The fighters were close to Mitch's plane.

Mitch keyed up the microphone again, not giving a care about radio discipline. "Dagger flight, what's the name of the lead?" Mitch asked.

"Sir, I'm Colonel Hainsworth," the fighter lead replied, trying to gauge the magnitude of the situation.

"Well fuck," Mitch accidentally blurted out, accidentally holding onto the transmit switch for the radios. Mitch's arms tingled with goosebumps after he realized that his expletive had been transmitted and put on record for everyone to hear.

"So much for professionalism over the radio," Mitch thought.

He sat back in his seat; the wind knocked right out of him. How could he have gone from the high in his flying career to now, one of the lowest?

"What the Hell has gotten into you? One minute you're happy as a clam, the next, you're a grumpy old man," Jim asked, not really understanding, or even caring, about the manic-depressive mood swings he was seeing from his captain.

Mitch's attitude soured significantly as he sat quietly before deciding to answer his co-pilot.

"This is the guy who handed me a rejection letter for a pilot spot over there. He did so with a Goddamn fucking smile on his face. He enjoys killing people's dreams. So now, I'll be a Technical Sargent until someone dies or retires, pushing fucking cargo for the rest of my military career," Mitch said with deep disappointment.

Mitch's explanation was cut short when the radio finally came back to life. "I'm going to guess that radio call wasn't meant for us?"

"Fuck," Mitch said out loud again as he rolled his eyes and not caring about choosing his words any longer.

"No, Colonel, just for you," Mitch said like the wind was just taken out of his sails. "You were the deciding factor on my pilot application to the one-twelfth."

"I was?" Hainsworth replied, not making the personal connection.

"Yes, this is Technical Sargent Mitch Bordoux," Mitch replied. "You smiled at me when you handed me a rejection letter, saying that my skillset wouldn't measure up to being a fighter pilot. You suggested I go and find a base to fly the heavies."

There was silence over the radio again, the Colonel obviously trying to make the mental connection. The embarrassment filtered through as radio silence. Mitch could only imagine what Hainsworth was saying under his breath.

The radio came to life again. "Took me a moment…the port dawg, air transportation guy?" Hainsworth replied, being somewhat casual over the radio.

"Yup, that's me," Mitch called over the radio.

"What the Hell are you doing up here? Trying to get a second interview?" Hainsworth asked, attempting to lighten the mood.

"I'm the left-seater here," Mitch replied, making sure that his surprise mention didn't ruin his chances of becoming any sort of Air Force pilot.

"Well, Jesus, if I would have known you were a 121 pilot, you would have been a shoe-in. Why didn't you bring that up?"

Mitch shook his head. "I did mention it in my bio, but I didn't highlight it because I was going to leave the airline gig for a chance to fly fighters, and I didn't want any preconceived notions about me."

"Well, Bordoux, that changes things. When we get on the ground, let's talk," Hainsworth said. "But for now, let's get to the bottom of this little problem first, shall we?"

Mitch said off-microphone sarcastically, "Yeah, so long as you don't blast us out of the sky first…" not really caring who, if anyone, heard his unnecessary comment.

Mitch's attention was quickly distracted from the unorthodox radio conversation by the sound of a couple loud pounds on the door.

"Why don't you two get a room when we land. Speaking of which, when are we landing?!" James shouted through the flight deck door. He was obviously listening to the conversation between Mitch and the guy who crashed his hopes of flying an F-16.

Behind the flight deck, in the cabin, James looked over at Jenny, who was carefully trying to fill the waste paper basket fill of random garbage. It didn't take long for James to catch on.

"What are you doing?" James asked as he stepped over to the waste paper basket.

Jenny's face shot up. To her surprise, James had been keeping an eye on her periodically throughout her odd bouts of activity.

"Cleaning up," Jenny replied hesitantly, startled after coming face-to-face with her hijacker.

Not really buying the "cleaning up" remark, James squinted one eye in an effort to identify if she was telling the truth or if she was hiding something.

"Move out of the way," James said, motioning his gun in a side-to-side manner, giving Jenny an opportunity to exit the immediate area.

"Wh-what?" Jenny asked.

"Move. Now," James said more demandingly.

Jenny bowed her head and stepped aside as James opened the secure compartment where the trash was located. The waste paper basket smelled like freshly brewed coffee where the spent coffee filters were located.

James pulled out a clear plastic bag which housed a lot of the other trash that Jenny and Wanda had collected over the first hour's snack and beverage service.

Within the trash can, an intentionally crumpled up piece of paper caught James eye. He looked up at Wanda and Jenny as he reached into the trash bag to retrieve the paper.

Wanda slowly made her way over to where Jenny stood. She placed her head near Jenny's ear and whispered, "Did the air marshals come on onboard?"

James unfolded the crumpled piece of paper from the trash and studied it, "Fed Air Marshal, 6C and 13A."

James' head rose slowly, realizing that the two flight attendants were trying to protect a couple armed passengers.

After glaring at the two flight attendants, James popped out his magazine on the handgun to check the remaining number of bullets. Satisfied that he had "enough" for 'a while', he then slammed the magazine back into the well of the handgun and walked by the two flight attendants.

"Thank you, ladies," James snarled as he stood behind the galley curtain, studying the first-class and economy classes of passengers.

The passengers were whimpering and crying at the stressful situation. Many of them had their heads down, as James commanded. A couple other passengers froze, watching James walk around the cabin like an emotionless madman. His eyes scanned the passengers, but his face as straight as a poker player trying to build his reputation on an impeccable bluff.

The man in 13B watched James study each passenger while looking at a piece of paper.

It was the same paper that the gate agent handed to Jenny before she boarded the flight.

Nervously, the man in 13B slowly grasped his firearm protectively. Limiting his motion, he concealed it in the seatback pocket, covering it with newspapers and a magazine.

James glanced down at the piece of paper again and then looked back up, scanning the coach cabin. He finally found seat 13A. It was empty.

His eyes narrowed back down at the wrinkled piece of paper, studied it again, and then shifted his focus to the occupied seat next to the empty 13A.

"Lucky you," James snickered to the man in 13B, referring to the unoccupied seat next to him that was meant for the Federal Air Marshal.

Satisfied that the air marshal wasn't in 13A after all, he trained his focus on the passengers in the first-class cabin, then in coach.

"6C," James said as he glanced over at the male and female sitting scared next to one another holding hands. The couple looked completely terrorized from the whole situation.

"Stand up!" James shouted at the gentleman who was gripping the woman's hand tightly.

"What?" the man asked, unsure of what was happening or, more importantly, why he was targeted.

"I said," James squinted his eyes and repeated himself slowly, "stand up, marshal."

James motioned his gun for the man to get out of the seat.

"Marshal?" the man asked, confused. "I-I don't know what you mean."

Jenny nervously stepped forward, trying to block James' advancement towards the man.

"He's telling the truth. He was assigned back in row 13 or something," Jenny pleaded. "The air marshals never came on board. One guy was late, so they never came on board," she rambled.

James ignored Jenny and looked back at the guy again. "Stand up. This is the last time I'm going to tell you."

The guy's mouth hung open and fumbled with his seatbelt as James grabbed him by his arm. When the man was finally able to manipulate the buckle for his seatbelt, he rose from the seat slowly.

"Please, I just wanted to sit next to my wife," the man motioned to the gorgeous woman next to him.

"Please," the man pleaded again.

"Where is your other cohort?" James asked.

"What cohort? I don't know what you're talking about!?" the man exclaimed as his hands fell out of their unfolded position, motioning and trying to be as submissive and non-confrontational as possible. "This is my wife!" the man stuttered, pleading for his life.

His wife sat beside them, petrified and speechless.

James pointed the gun at the man's chest, right around the region of his heart. The smell of sweat and fear permeated throughout the first-class cabin.

The man's wife finally spoke up, crying out, "Andy, come back. That's my husband!" She tried getting out of her seat, but her rubbery legs weren't making movement easy within the first-class seats.

"13A, the seat is empty. Where is your other team member?" James snarled at the man.

The man once again pleaded that he had no idea what James was talking about.

James grabbed the man and dragged him to the middle of the aisle, the gun pointed directly at the man's head.

"Where are you, marshal?!" James asked, in the most intimidating voice he could muster.

The passengers stared at the black polymer-framed gun trained at the back of the middle-aged man, who had obviously and very quickly made his peace with his maker.

Wanda came up behind James and tugged on his shirt, breaking James' attention from the terrified man, crying, "He's telling you the truth, that man couldn't find a seat next to his wife. The air marshals never came onboard, and he took their spot!"

James stood for a second taking in the expressions of the various passengers who were obviously scared for their lives, reacting to a traumatic situation as one would expect.

Some of the passengers were crying, others were praying, but the majority of the passengers were paralyzed by fear. Mothers and fathers covered their children's eyes and ears. Most people were visibly shaking out of fear while others were rocking from side to side.

James paused for a split second, but then looked back at Wanda, and replied coolly, "I don't believe you."

Without hesitation, James pulled the trigger of the larger framed pistol, and the gun's rack snapped back, ejecting the spent casing. The chemical reaction propelled the bullet through the muzzle of the gun, embedding itself into the back of the man.

The man flopped onto the floor, the gunshot killing him almost instantaneously. As the passengers watched and plugged their ears over the report of the gun's loud bark, one thing was obvious: everything was occurring in slow motion.

A loud bang echoed throughout the cabin again as the man laid face-down in the aisle. The carpet turned dark red as the fibers became overly saturated in blood.

Behind the flight deck door, Mitch and Jim were startled by all the unknown commotion on the other side of them.

"Jesus Christ," Jim finally said, knowing full well that the explosive bang indicated another person being shot dead.

The smell of spent gunpowder was pushed through the cabin ventilation system yet again as the air circulated and recirculated.

The man's wife screamed at the top of her lungs, "Nooo!" as she lunged towards her husband's lifeless body.

The man's wife cried uncontrollably as James bent down and went through the man's pockets and personal documents, finally finding his boarding pass and identification.

James knelt down and held the driver's license and the boarding pass up against the lights of the cabin overhead lights.

He compared the boarding pass with the seat assignment. The seat assignment didn't match with what was on the boarding pass.

The wife of the now dead man glared up at James, cursing the man who had killed her husband. James paid no attention to her, stepping around her. There was no feeling and no look of remorse from James.

Jenny and Wanda stood frozen, like they were permanent fixtures or statues onboard the aircraft, unable to move due to shock of what they just witnessed.

James continued to dig through the dead man's belongings.

"Retired police officer?" James said, pulling up and showing the man's identification, stamped as "retired" on it. "Looks like you were telling the truth, miss flight attendant," James snarled, his attention brought away from the sobbing wife, who held her husband's head and body in her arms.

Eyes all over the cabin glared at James as he asserted dominance once again, waving his gun around like he was anything but a pro at the whole impromptu hijacking thing.

Meanwhile, in the flight deck, Mitch and Jim reported the commotion in the back through the radio, making sure that the events would be captured one way or the other when the aircraft called out "SELCAL," alerting the crew that a message had arrived from dispatch.

Quickly, Mitch looked up the message response from his query regarding Federal Air Marshal onboard.

It read, "Negative, they were delayed and had other flights booked for later in the afternoon in St. Louis."

"Well fuck," Mitch said, reading the message out loud, after he took the time to read the message in his head.

"We are all alone up here," Jim replied, making sure the words marinated.

Chapter 6
Nor'easter 1172, In flight,
East of Dayton, Ohio

James strolled around the forward galley after coming down from his adrenaline high after taking over an airliner and killing five people. He took his time and moved through all of the galley catering carts.

"What the fuck is this?" James asked, annoyed with the lack of food onboard the aircraft.

"What, you were expecting a five-course meal? It'll be your last meal before you meet your maker," Wanda said sarcastically while she grinded her teeth, her jaw clenched, trying to show her ultimate contentment and disgust.

Jenny saw the pain in Wanda's eyes and pulled her away. "It's okay. We'll be down on the ground in a couple hours, and we'll be safe. This guy will get what's coming to him," Jenny said, recognizing that it was probably the first time that nearly everyone onboard had ever seen anyone get killed. For many, it was a firsthand experience that they would unfortunately remember forever.

Going through all the cubbies, James came across the required medical kit, then the flight attendant's bags, and eventually, the last stop was the obscure liquor cabinet.

James' eyes grew huge when he saw the nearly endless supply of rum and vodka. He looked around as his tingly senses tugged at his desire for having a drink or two.

Again, James looked around to see if anyone was watching him indulge. Naturally, there were always passengers keeping their eyes open and looking around, but the feeling of being watched didn't bother him as much as he struggled with the decision on whether or not to take a sip.

"Fuck," James said as he swung open the liquor cabinet door again.

The bottles clanked against one another, protesting the turbulence. The distinct sounds of glass against glass could even be heard over the dull roar of the engines.

Wendy and Jenny watched in horror as James grabbed a couple shooters, ripped the tops off them, and proceeded to slam each shooter, one after another, until four empty bottles were sitting on the cart.

James braced his hand against the galley cart, mentally preparing himself for the shock of the burning sensation that usually came with ingesting hard liquor.

"What are you looking at?" James questioned the flight attendants. "Haven't you ever seen someone drink real stuff before?"

"Losers," James muttered to himself at the thought of the flight attendants not being able to keep up with his drinking.

Jenny and Wanda were both highly disgusted, but knew one of two things were going to happen. One, he could get incapacitated by booze, in which they could regain control of the situation. The second option was more dangerous: he could get even more unpredictable and violent.

It didn't take long before the booze started to kick in. The dehydrated state of flying in general allowed for the rum to get digested in James' bloodstream quicker than if he was well-hydrated and nourished.

"Fuck," James slipped out again as he felt a slight pounding in his head coming on, which was abnormal from his regular drinking routines.

He staggered over to Jenny, who was somewhat blocking the flight deck door. The smell of sweat and terrible body odor wafted from his clothes. His breath reeked of alcohol, and his eyes were full of fire and somewhat bloodshot as the rum began taking over his circulatory system.

"Get them to open the door. Don't you have keys to the flight deck?" James quizzed Jenny.

"No," Jenny said defiantly.

"No what?" James inquired again.

"No to both. I don't have keys and I'm not going to get the door open even if you kill us all. It's. Not. Going. To. Happen," Jenny said sternly and defiantly.

A loudly professed "FUCK!" shook the whole cabin to its core when James threw a temper tantrum because he wasn't getting his way. The jet wasn't descending like what had been a large complaint.

"If you're not going to open it, I will," James said, highly convinced that he could and would find a way to break through the reinforced flight deck door.

Wanda looked over at James, who had waltzed over and taken a seat on the forward-most flight attendant jump seat. His eyes looked like he was thinking hard, pondering about something.

"What the Hell happened to you?" Wanda asked, trying to make some sort of connection with James.

James looked up and waved his hand, "Get the fuck away from me, bitch," James said in a snide tone, completely dismissing her attempt.

"You mean to tell me that you don't give two shits as to what you're putting innocent people through? These people never cheated on you," Wanda said with her hands folded out, trying to be as non-threatening as she knew. She also knew that bringing up his past failed love history and murders could potentially aggravate James even more.

"Cheated?" James shot back. "Nobody ever cheated on me. You need to stop watching the news. Now, get the fuck away from me," he said as his eyes opened up.

Wanda glanced in James' eyes, as she could see the fire burning within his soul and the amount of pain he felt, but the emotional toll of caring wasn't a part of the equation today.

Just as Wanda turned, she rolled her eyes and began to make her way towards the first-class cabin, when James spoke up again.

"The fuck do you know about being cheated on?" James snarled as he got to his feet.

"Oh, a thing or two," Wanda said, un-phased by his heated temper, and not even turning around to acknowledge the man.

"Oh really? How about this, you ever know how to deal with this?" James asked as he cocked his arm back, the bottom of the pistol clearly present with his intended aim.

James swung the pistol across Wanda's face, but instead of nailing her in the face with the blunter side of the bottom of the grip, James swiped the barrel. The front side clipped Wanda in her cheek as the gun moved swiftly, at the control of James.

Wanda's face shot back, the momentum of the pistol's kinetic energy straining her neck. She fell to the ground, shocked and sobbing, before one of the passengers in the first row got to his feet and helped Wanda care for her wound.

While she was being cared for, James snickered and casually walked back to the booze cart and grabbed a few more shooters of alcohol. It was almost like he couldn't help himself.

Dribbles of blood from Wanda's cheek made it look worse than it was, for it was just a cut to her cheek and nothing more serious.

The jet encountered more turbulence as they passed over the large city of Columbus.

The turbulence caused significant rattling, which originated from the galley catering carts. The latches keeping the catering carts locked up were not engaged, which allowed the carts to roll out of their stowage positions and propped themselves against the thin wall that divided the galley from the passenger compartment.

James looked at the catering carts, the thin profile allowing for maximum contents. There were three carts altogether; two were newer carts, and an older cart had a previous airline logo on it.

The door of the older cart managed to pop its lock and swing open. The shaken carbonated beverages rattled in unison within their trays.

The turbulence was getting progressively worse as the jet plugged away closer and closer to storm cells. The up and down drafts caused a secondary, strong feeling of unease within the jet.

Propping his hand against the heavier cart, James sloppily pushed the other two carts back in their holes, latching the arms in the locking position, making sure they didn't come back out.

By this point, James was already heavily intoxicated. His speech had begun to make less coherent sentences.

James struggled to stand up straight with the turbulence, but his reaction time lagged when trying to compensate with the fluctuations and fell face first into the aisle of the plane.

"Why don't you come and sit down," Jenny said, tugging at James' sleeve after watching him stagger back to his feet while pushing the carts in the holes.

James shot a disgusted look over to Jenny, who watched, un-empathetic to James' challenges. "Fuck you," was all he could muster as he located the large bottles of water, where he proceeded to rip the cap off the top and began drinking a quarter of the large half-gallon jug of water.

Fed up with the turbulence, James sat down in the galley, and braced his back against the galley carts in an effort to stabilize himself.

Frustrated that people were not listening or understanding him, James got back to his feet after sitting, unsure how he actually got onto his knees, and grabbed the one cart that he hadn't put back in its cubby.

He excessively gripped the heavier cart, its rollers aged from years of abuse from all the different crews, turbulence, and catering companies.

The older carts were made from a steel frame and had some significant weight behind them.

As he was moving it, James readjusted his grip. The cart's squeaky wheels really didn't lend itself to stealthy movement, as everyone heard it moving around the cabin.

James rolled the cart all the way back to row six, where first-class cabins ended and economy seating started. It was pretty much a straight-shot to the flight deck door, and with any luck, he would be able to force the jet down once he got the flight deck door open.

"Never mess with a man who doesn't have anything left to lose!" James grunted as he lunged forward, his drunken legs pushing the cart with maximum effort as they could, allowing the cart to gain speed as it rolled quickly down the aisle.

Passengers were startled by the sight of a drunk man, who doubled as their hijacker, shoving a cart down the aisle. Any stray feet or legs left dangling in the aisle meant they would be run over as the cart barreled past.

The squeaking sounds of the cart's wheels were heard by both Mitch and Jim inside the flight deck, but there was not much they could do. They had already put the flight deck jump seat out and latched it for ensured security. The setup was identical to the flight attendant jump seat, just on the other side of the door.

The squeaking of the wheels came closer and closer, the turbulence aiding its sheer momentum. Suddenly, a loud metal on metal crash jostled the two pilots as the cart slammed into the center of the door.

The door shook and jostled, but held firm. A large crease in the door gave testament to two things: the cart was heavy, but the door was strong.

"Jesus fucking Christ!" Mitch shouted from the left seat.

The crash of the cart ramming into the door immediately triggered a flashback.

It jolted Mitch back to his time in Afghanistan, with a distinct sound of a 107mm rocket whizzing past his head. The combination of the screeching wheels rolling on the carpet along the aisle and the impact of the cart crashing into the door, paralleled the environmental conditions he experienced in a previous more traumatizing part of his life.

Mitch sat paralyzed in his seat as his mind continued to roll the reel from his past, exposing his possible PTSD experience from years ago.

Mitch was in the Air National Guard in Ohio in a logistics capacity. His job was to load and unload cargo and passengers to and from aircraft that just landed, either stateside or down range, in a deployed setting.

Mitch could still smell the dust in the air. It was a fine dust that gave the sun a beautiful sunrise each morning.

Mitch was admiring the picture of the sun rising over the eastern peak when he saw a dim flash coming from the mountainside. He didn't really pay much attention to it, as it was common sight for dust particles to react with light in such a way that it played tricks on your eyes.

After being in awe of the scenery, Mitch returned to his teammates, doing most of the work.

"*Errr errr errr*... Incoming incoming incoming... *errr errr err*... Incoming incoming incoming."

The buzz-saw sound of the base defense weapon system firing its 3,000 rounds per minute was forever etched in Mitch's memory.

"Incoming incoming incoming," the alarm sounded again.

Mitch hit the dirt, chest first, adrenaline pulsing through his veins. He remembered to wrap his hands around his head, covering his ears.

"Get down!" Mitch yelled as he looked up at his two other friends, who had their eyes to the sky.

Suddenly, the whole world slowed to a snail's pace as chunks of concrete, dirt, and dust became airborne, and an ear-bursting blast enveloped the three men.

Mitch was on the ground with his fingers in his ears and his mouth wide open, ingesting earthy Afghan dust and dirt.

The percussive blast almost immediately caused ringing in his ears as he got to his knees looking around, stunned by the shockwave that enveloped him moments prior.

As Mitch got to his feet, he looked around again, searching for his two colleagues while dust and dirt sprinkled over him like pelting rain drops. It was traumatic and heightened Mitch's senses to an extreme measure. He was even able to feel the impact of each pebble that struck him and smelled the distinct scent of spent ordinance and melting metal.

Mitch looked around frantically searching, until he eventually found the bloody body of his teammate Charlie Zerwas, who laid motionless on the ground, his uniform soaked in dark red blood.

Mitch grabbed Charlie by his t-shirt and jacket, laid him on the ground, and instantly performed first aid on his wingman until first responders arrived, slapping him several times before he snapped out of his haze.

Mitch suddenly snapped back to the present inside the jet, jolted by a firm slap to his right shoulder.

"Hey, are you going to get that?" Jim asked, trying to snap Mitch out of his daze with a second friendly, but firm, slap to the face.

Mitch looked over at Jim, who cocked his arm back, ready to administer another come-to-Jesus moment for his captain.

"Mitch, you with me?" Jim shouted, confident he was mentally back.

"Wh-what? Yeah, I'm here," Mitch said in a cold sweat, somehow feeling somewhat agitated.

"Where are you?" Jim shouted.

"Get off my back," Mitch snarled, still in a hazy daze.

"Eleven Seventy-two, Chicago Center, you up on frequency?" the controller called up.

Inundated with sensory overload, Mitch prioritized the cabin call versus the controller calling the hijacked jet.

The cabin call button chimed again in the flight deck again.

On the other side of the flight deck door, Jenny sat the interphone back in its cradle again after a second failed attempt at reaching the captain.

She reached over and grabbed the galley catering cart that was used as a failed battering ram. As she pulled the cart from its resting place against the flight deck door, she then replaced it back in the compartment, securing it with red levers. Giving the carts a quick tug, she ensured that the turbulence wouldn't hurt anything else.

Jenny looked around her shoulder as she was making sure all the carts were stowed, while James was busy walking up and down the aisle.

As Jenny refocused her attention towards the carts, she snuck over to one of the compartments onboard the jet. She unlatched one of the doors, the one with the personal phones located inside.

Taking a quick glance towards James, she took a deep breath and opened the phone that Mitch had seen earlier in the morning, the same one she had semi-voluntarily shown him when demanded before the flight took off.

Jenny sat down composing a message on her main phone to Mitch, making sure the settings allowed easy access.

James was still pacing back and forth in the cabin. He had already made one lap up and down the aisle.

With the initial shock and commotion settling, James was busy looking around, becoming increasingly agitated. It seemed that he was getting worked up at nothing, almost as if he was paranoid about something in particular.

James looked like a normal person, maybe even handsome in some regards. He had short blond hair which had been cut. It was a matter of ease. His voice was low and gravelly, almost to the point of being gruff. He didn't look like a maniac killer that the news portrayed him to be.

However, with him hijacking a jet, it was clear to the passengers that looks could be deceiving.

James glanced toward a male passenger, a banker from lower Manhattan, on his way to visit a client in St. Louis.

The look on James' face was surprisingly pleasant, almost friendly, obviously a side effect of the particular mental condition that he had suffered from.

The male passenger finally got up from his seat and walked towards James. The man's eyes focused intently on James as well as his gun.

Wanda watched the whole situation unfold from a first row seat while she recovered from getting violently pistol-whipped by James.

The banker approached James. While getting closer, he took off his blazer and demanded that the guy release the passengers.

"You know this isn't going to end well for you." The banker said calmly, "Give me the gun and let us go."

James chuckled at the pitiful attempt to broker a peaceful ending to the impromptu hijacking.

James brought his gun up to shoulder level, and the banker carefully put his hand on the top of the slide and pushed on the barrel, diverting it from what would have been a lethal shot.

"What the fuck is wrong with you? Did you short wire or something when you were a kid?" the banker yelled, trying another tactic.

"Why don't you just go and sit down with everyone else," James said quietly, not overly worried about the man.

"I will not. You're holding us hostage. You're surely going to die today," the banker replied, studying the nervous tick that James started to exhibit when being pushed.

James, unable to maintain his full balance, used the turbulence to gently prop himself up with the edge of an empty seat back, his eyes glaring at the banker.

"You want me to let everyone go? How about the fucking captain lands this fucking jet, then *you'll* be free to go."

"Have you looked outside? Do you think he can land in *that*?!" the banker asked, pointing out the window, showing that the storms blocked any sort of direct flight to their destination.

"Fucking just sit down!" James snarled as he dropped the aim of the gun a bit lower.

A loud bone-shattering bang, followed with a bright flash of expanding, igniting gunpowder, shoved the ballistically-twisting piece of lead through the air, until it embedded into the banker's stomach.

The banker fell to the floor as he gripped his stomach, which was quickly getting saturated in blood.

James looked at another passenger and said, "Get him back in his seat," pointing at the banker's crumpled body.

As James continued walking down the aisle, he faced each of the passengers with his eyes fiery, shouting in a slurred voice, "FUCK ALL OF YOU. WE'RE GONNA CRASH AND WE'RE ALL GONNA DIE! DEAL WITH IT."

He then looked around and added, "You better make your plans while you can!"

The sharpness of James' words pierced all possible morals that any of the passengers had at the prospect of getting down safely.

Jenny, who had eventually pulled her jump seat out of its stowed position, sat down, worked her busy hands and arms through the four-point harness, and continued to construct a message to Mitch.

Jenny sat in her crew seat with tears rolling down her cheeks. She added onto the message as ideas continued to flood her mind. When she was done, she took the second cellphone and texted Jim that she had informed the Human Resources department as well as Mitch of what happened.

Jenny's mind continued playing the situation out in her mind, which brought her to another low, as if she somehow was responsible for the world's problems. It was almost like one thing led to another, and that none of her passengers would have been in this situation if she hadn't committed wrongdoings.

Jenny hadn't felt this way for years. She found herself subconsciously scratching her wrists again, where she flashed back to her time in the Marines.

Nothing much comforted Jenny, especially post-deployment. When she returned home, she suffered from survivor's guilt after her tower collapsed and her battle buddy didn't survive. Depressed with the knowledge of what happened, coupled with a few months of heavy drinking and anti-anxiety drugs to cope with the loss (which the Veterans' Affairs so generously provided), she locked herself into the bathroom of her base's living quarters and found a razor.

Jenny sat on the toilet cover, deeply pondering her next actions. It was probably the first time in her life that she had no thoughts in her mind to help guide her.

It didn't take long before Jenny's roommate came home after a shortened trip to the local Walmart. She found Jenny's body lying in a pool of blood with the sink water running.

"Let me be," Jenny muttered to her roommate as she cried.

Jenny snapped back to reality in the jet cabin. She looked down at her bloody fingers. She had scratched her scars deep enough that they had started to bleed again.

A man, sitting in 2A, looked around for where the hijacker was located. Watching the hijacker and taking a chance, he got up from his seat and cautiously stepped over to where Jenny had been sitting. She was obviously not in the right frame of mind to have a cheesy conversation.

"Let me help you with that. I'm Derek," the man replied with a slight smile, offering to help fix the bleeding.

Jenny, feeling embarrassed, hadn't realized she was sitting in front of everyone, losing her mind during a hijacking. She had only hoped that nobody else noticed.

"You were in the war," Derek observed, trying to bring Jenny into the now, versus living in the past.

Jenny wiped the tears from her eyes and nodded softly and gently, acknowledging Derek's question.

"I was in the war, too," Derek said, trying to be gentle with the scratches, as to not cause more pain or issues.

James made his way back towards the front of the airplane when he noticed Derek and Jenny congregating in the front galley of the jet.

An irate James marched up to Jenny and Derek, his eyes flaring up with the fire in his stomach.

"Get back to your seat!" James shouted to Derek, who had turned around just in time to see James hovering over the two of them.

James' eyes were dark, and it was worrying for Jenny… even more so when James pulled the handgun out again and pointed it between Derek's eyes.

"Don't make me ask you again. Get up and go back to your seat," James growled.

Derek got up and shuffled over to his original seat, 2A.

"No, you know what, go back into a row further back and find an empty seat," James said, trying to keep congregating passengers from one another.

Derek looked at James confused as to the logic of putting him in the back, but complied nonetheless.

Chapter 7
Nor'easter 1172, In flight,
Above Dayton, Ohio
09:05 a.m.

James watched carefully as Derek took his new seat in row 13, in the back and over the wing. Derek was dressed in a nice suit jacket and slacks with no tie. He was very non-descript looking for a military guy, especially when everyone talked about the haircut.

Satisfied that Derek was in a seat farther away, James turned around and stood over Jenny for a few moments. Jenny's heart pumped forcefully, adrenaline coursing through her bloodstream. She had regained some of her composure after her emotional meltdown, wiping more tears from her eyes, which now exposed her face as her makeup disappeared through the blood, sweat, and tears.

Her passengers saw her as she was, just like one of them: a passenger held hostage by a madman.

Everyone sat in relative silence. There were some passengers that were praying, others were just trying to make themselves comfortable, and the rest were trying to connect to the Wi-Fi on their phones. Mostly everyone in the cabin had the same idea: to send what they thought would be their final messages to their loved ones on the ground.

James walked slowly back down towards the back of the jet, and then again towards the front. However, when he turned around, a proverbial "lightbulb" came on in his head. He stood in place for a few moments and waited.

Shortly after confirming what he was feeling, James walked past Wanda, who was seated in one of the empty first-class seats, and then up to Jenny, who had been eyeing James pacing up and down the aisle.

"Why are we not descending?" James asked, glaring over at Jenny, expecting a fearful reaction from the emotionally vulnerable flight attendant.

"I don't know, I'm not flying the jet," Jenny scowled at her captor, as she stood up. The look in her eyes showed a sort of internal numbness. She really felt like her own prisoner, and she had nothing left to lose now.

"Call the cockpit and find out," James demanded, his eyes narrowing and darkening.

Jenny felt the sense that James wanted someone to challenge him. He was taunting her, implying that she wasn't strong enough or had as much willpower as he did to commit a dreadful act of defiance.

Jenny took a deep breath and nodded, finally holding onto the spare ounce of hope that she just might actually get through this. She rang the flight deck in an effort to reach out and gather more information about when and where they'd be landing.

James had been sitting and listening to the one-sided conversation from the flight deck crew. The information was spotty as expected, and the delay tactic was all too familiar with him.

Jenny finally hung up the phone and looked at James, his eyes showing a burning fire that was just waiting for some gasoline.

"Well?" James asked.

"You heard what I heard..." Jenny said sarcastically, not really willing to give James any sort of knowing or unknowing advantage.

"Call the captain again," James said persuasively, "and if he gives us what we want to hear, then you'll live through this."

Jenny's stomach sank, the wind knocked out of her sails, knowing that she surely wasn't going to live through the whole event.

Everything that happened from thereon out was based on this next conversation with the man who believed she cheated on him with his own co-pilot. It was a debilitating dilemma to comprehend.

While Jenny took a couple moments to think about the whole situation, she took a couple deep breaths, trying to find intestinal fortitude.

As she stood in the galley, James turned and walked back to one of the passengers who he had seen before, something piqued his interest.

The kid was playing with his survival bracelet, which was tied together with a long and continuous strand of paracord.

"Give me your bracelet," James demanded, looking down at the kid. James was certainly a madman, but the wheels were turning in his psychotic head.

The 15-year old kid contemplated on refusing to fuel his inner desire to be a troublemaker, but then reluctantly obliged.

Jenny picked up the interphone and thought for another moment. What would she say? Was James even extending an olive branch, or was it just a ploy, and they were *all* going to die?

James returned to the galley with a bracelet dangling from his free hand. He stood in front of the door, studying its mechanics.

"This door isn't bigger than the hole, like all these other doors," James said cautiously.

Jenny glanced over at the door, knowing the answer, but reluctant to say anything.

"What did the captain say?" James asked as he began untying the bracelet.

The bracelet was an olive-green kind with about 20 feet of 550 cord, also known as paracord. It was a strong material with a tinsel strength of over 500 pounds.

"You were saying?" James said again.

"I didn't talk to him," Jenny finally said.

James looked Jenny over as he retorted, "What a shame."

He continued playing with the cord. He fashioned a loop on one end, then walked up to the passenger service door. The door was located on the front left side of the jet. It was a heavy-duty construction. It was different than the rest of the doors on the jet, which were held in place by a latch and pressure, called plug doors. The doors were larger than the holes they covered.

The passenger door, however, was only held in place by cam-locks. The plug type doors were impossible to open in flight because of the pressure differences between the inside and outside.

The passenger door only required the handle to be lifted up from its stowed position and then the door would open up, regardless of the jet being pressurized or unpressurized.

James tied the fashioned loop over the door handle of the passenger door. He then routed the loose end of the cord through a couple handles, which were built into the bulkhead, allowing the upward motion to unlatch the door.

Jenny looked at the whole setup, as she instantly knew what the plan was. A distinct feeling of dread overwhelmed her. There was no going home, there was no safe landing… just a few seconds of useful consciousness before the jet broke up and sucked everyone out.

"Wh-what are you doing?" Jenny asked nervously.

"What does it look like? The pilots don't want to land, so I'm going to force the landing," James replied, extremely pleased with his idea.

"B-but you can't open the door in flight," Jenny said, trying to sound convincing.

"No? Are you sure?" James asked, challenging Jenny to a debate as to why she was wrong.

"Look, let me call the flight deck again," Jenny said as she motioned towards the handheld device, while simultaneously pressing the call button.

"Flight deck," Mitch responded cautiously as Jenny called again. He had already tried to shake her dooming prediction from her head.

"Why are we not on the ground?" Jenny asked firmly.

"Weather," Mitch answered gruffly, holding onto the previous conversation as a benchmark on how he was the captain, and he was still in charge of the aircraft.

James broke into the conversation.

"That's bullshit, I can see the ground everywhere. It's green farmlands and small cities. I can see airports all over the place!" he barked.

"Exactly, they are small airports that we cannot land at. We're too big, we'd crash! And unless you want to die, let us handle the flying, and you go and fuck off. We're going to get you into St. Louis like you originally wanted," Mitch said firmly.

"Are you getting smart with me?" James said, sensing the high levels of contempt from the flight deck.

James handed the intercom handset back to Jenny, who had already mentally snapped.

"Tell the captain to get us on the ground, or else I pull the cord," James scowled in Jenny's direction.

Jenny fumbled with the phone and she dropped the hand piece. She quickly retrieved the receiver and brought it up to her ear again, with James listening.

"Look, if he wants to land right now, why doesn't he just fucking jump out of the airplane," Mitch said, severely annoyed that his now-perfect airline career was dead, and that he didn't give an honest care in the world.

"Mitch, what the fuck, man?" Jenny overheard Jim shoot back at Mitch over the intercom.

An audible click of a gun's hammer cocking back to the firing position made Jenny's hair on the back of her neck stand up. She turned around to come face-to-face with the blackened barrel of the handgun that had been pointed right at her.

"That was a very bad choice of words, Captain," James replied in a soft and calm voice. His voice was eerily different.

"O-oh no... H-he's got the gun to my head... p-please just get us on the ground!" Jenny said softly, whimpering.

In the flight deck, Jim glared over at Mitch in a way that he was seriously contemplating taking over the flight and the role as the captain instead of Mitch. In Jim's opinion, Mitch was handling the whole hijacking very poorly until this point.

"Dude, we need to get onto the ground and save these people," Jim finally said, chiming into the conversation, ignoring any ancillary details.

"Let me run this show!" Mitch snarled at Jim. "I'm the captain here, and I'm in charge. We're flying to St. Louis, where we will be handed off to seasoned negotiators, and *maybe* we might just live!" Mitch yelled, infuriated at Jim for questioning his judgment.

"Mitch, listen to me. It's Jenny on the line. She loves you and you love her," Jim said.

Mitch snarled back at Jim, like a dog that had been poked too many times. "Don't you *ever* mix professional vs. personal lives in your work. What Jenny and I had is between *us*, unless someone like you comes along and sticks his new dick in her before you're even out of training!"

Jim, taken aback by the harsh comments, squinted his eyes at Mitch, contemplating what his next words would be.

"Yeah, I didn't think you had anything left to say," Mitch said, trying to put the final nail in the coffin, which was almost too painful for Mitch to acknowledge in addition to being hijacked.

"It's not what you think, Mitch," Jim finally blurted back.

"Oh, it's not?" Mitch asked. "So, what you're going to tell me is that it was all your fault, where you drugged her on one of your trips… which, in that case, would make you a rapist. Is that what you're trying to say?"

"You know what, Mitch, fuck you, and fuck her. She deserves someone better than you, anyway," Jim shot back, defensively angry. Mitch's words struck a nerve.

Jenny sat in the flight attendant jump seat in the forward galley, James' gun pointed at her. The seat was conveniently placed where the flight deck door couldn't be opened, even from the inside, if the seat was installed and latched. She listened, along with James, to the back and forth between Mitch and Jim. Each time that her name was brought up, it was a proverbial kick in the gut.

Finally, Jenny got on her feet and stowed the jump seat back in its little cubby.

She made a tight fist and hammered repeatedly on the door crying out, "Get this plane on the fucking ground, or we're all dead!"

There was no response from the flight deck. Jenny was exhausted from lashing out, all of her emotional angst boiling to the surface.

James watched in silence, amused from the comfort of the galley.

Jenny turned and glanced over at her first-class passengers, many of whom were shocked and crying at the emotional sight of Jenny's breakdown of professionalism.

Calming herself down again, she grabbed the intercom again and punched in the button, connecting to the flight deck.

"Flight deck," Mitch answered immediately.

"It's Jenny," she said in a more controlled voice, but still slightly crying.

"What has gotten into you, Jenny?" Mitch said. "You know the procedure. Remain in control as best as you can and let us get the jet down."

"Yeah, while you and Jim go run off from the escape hatch in there!" Jenny shot back.

"What's going on, Jenny?" Mitch asked in a monotone voice that somewhat resembled a parallel question of, "Why are you bothering us again?"

"He wants us on the ground. When are we getting on the ground?!" Jenny asked again, knowing full well that she was poking a bear.

There was silence between the two crew members until Jenny finally broke the silence with an unorthodox, "I love you."

James glared at Jenny and sneered at the inopportune showing of affection.

At that point, he *knew* he held the key to whether or not Jenny would live, and the thought maniacally delighted him.

Mitch heard heavy breathing over the intercom.

"Tell him…" Mitch paused for a second, after his mind registered the magnitude of what was just said to him.

But before he could say another thing, the sound of the interphone getting ripped from Jenny's hands could be heard during the struggle. A crying Jenny was heard saying, "Tell Jim to tell you what happened…" Jenny cried in the background.

James hushed Jenny as he put the interphone up to his ear, and said, "Captain, we had a deal… Get this plane on the ground."

Mitch rolled his eyes and said, "There was no deal. I cannot just land a jet this size on just ANY old fucking runway. If you want us to land on an air force base, you'll be captured when the wheels touch the ground. If you want us to run off the runway and kill everyone on board, we aren't doing that either. If you want to die, you have a gun, do it yourself, for fuck's sake!" Mitch snarled, then disconnected the connection.

Jim's head shot over to Mitch's direction. His face took on a severely deep red at the captain's response to the call.

Mitch remained emotionless and a far cry from the captain the day prior. His bottom lip was quivering as his mind chewed on the emotions that were going through his brain and heart.

On the other side of the flight deck door in the galley, James stood in the galley, next to the service door, which was directly across from the main entrance.

He held the interphone facing Jenny as he raised the handgun to Jenny's face once again and demanded, "Call him again. One more time."

Jenny, shaking, complied as she punched in the code to reach the flight deck once again. A loud gasp from Jenny was audible on the other side of the intercom once the connection was made. The gasp was involuntary, as Jenny's eyes grew large staring down the dark pipe, again, that was the black barrel of the handgun point pointed back at her face.

"Oh my God!" Jenny cried out in a shaky voice. The smell of nervous sweat wafted throughout the immediate area.

"Open the door!" Jenny finally demanded.

Inside the fight deck, Jim shouted, "Jesus fuck, you're going to just let her die?!"

Mitch's face soured significantly. Mentally, he was weighing two terrible options. The first option was to comply and open the door, thus saving Jenny's immediate life. The second option was making the gamble on Jenny's life that their hijacker was bluffing and thus remaining in control of the jet.

"We cannot open that door. You remember what happened back in 2001, right?" Mitch said sternly, affirming his decision.

"She's going to DIE!" Jim yelped out, protesting at how Mitch had been handling the whole event from the very beginning.

"We don't know what's going on through that door. All the passengers could already be dead, for all we know. We are NOT going to open that fucking door!" Mitch snarled.

Fed up with Mitch's handling of the situation, Jim's fingers quickly found the heavy-duty buckle for the harness. He quickly twisted his quick release harness buckle, thus releasing the straps. He launched backwards out of his seat with his arm fully extended in a bold attempt to unlatch the secured flight deck door. His hand came within an inch of grabbing the deadbolt, holding the door locked.

While Jim launched himself, he shoved the left rudder pedal all the way down, causing the jet to yaw to the left violently, and the chirping of the autopilot disengaging filled the flight deck.

"Jim, no!" Mitch cried out.

Everything within the jet jostled and became airborne.

As the jet went sideways, pitched, and rolled, a whole host of overhead bins snapped open, dropping their contents onto the passengers below. The shrieks and screams demonstrated the sheer panic and chaos that had already been planted with the hijacking.

With the jet pitching and rolling from the obnoxious unintended input from Jim, Mitch reached out his hand like a viper and grabbed Jim's waist and a leg as he was flying by.

The fear of Jim's actions was almost instantaneous, and Mitch did what he had to in order to prevent the first officer from making a bad situation even worse.

Mitch's grip on Jim wasn't strong enough to really attempt a prevention of a violation of federal laws, after all.

With Mitch grasping at whatever he could of Jim's body, which wasn't much, Jim reached around and nailed Mitch in the temple twice with his ring finger, digging his knuckles into the side of Mitch's left eyebrow.

Mitch jumped back, retreating from the stinging pain before twisting his quick release harness to pursue Jim.

"Jim, no!!!" Mitch cried out again as Jim grabbed hold of the metal latch and jolted it open, allowing the flight deck door to fly open in the middle of the chaos that ensued in front of the flight deck door.

Just as the flight deck door flew open, James pulled the trigger of the handgun which was trained on Jenny, almost as if he was lining up this cold-blooded kill for the perfect moment.

A loud gunshot pierced their ears as the smell of spent gun powder wafted throughout the immediate area, and the empty casing bounced harmlessly along the floor of the galley, giving a muffled dinging sound.

A shocked Jim stopped cold in his tracks as James turned to his side, looking at the first officer who had just magically appeared.

Jim was now only four or five feet away. As he stood right in the frame of the flight deck door, his eyes told the tale that he instantly regretted his actions.

Jim took a large gasp while muttering, "Oh my God," not having more then that split second to acknowledge the obvious.

Meanwhile, Mitch was beyond shocked, trying to quickly take in all the visual information he could. He glanced over Jim's shoulder and noticed a rope that had been strung across from the main entrance door, ending where James stood, on the other side of the jet.

A slight smile crept over James' face. Jim found the paracord *just* as James pulled it tight.

With a strong, fluid motion, he yanked on the rope, which was tied to the door handle. The handle jumped up like it was under spring tension, unseating the stowing handle for the passenger door. The door's cam-locks instantly rotated, allowing the door to pop open. The whole hunk of metal, known as the boarding door, entered the slipstream of the jet.

Time slowed to a glacial pace as the swift air caught the previously recessed door's edges and sucked the entire door out of the hole that it was locked in place with. Its cam-locks no longer secured the door to the airframe, allowing it to freely open.

In the flight deck, a red light flashed, along with an audible "DOOR" and "cabin pressure" alerts.

The main passenger door, battling against the wind, jolted open and an instant haze enveloped the entire cabin. The fog that instantly appeared was also accompanied with a painful, ear-piercing pressure change. It felt like an instant sinus infection or diving into a deep pool.

The pressure change also meant that everything that wasn't nailed down and secured became airborne and was sucked out of the gaping hole of the airplane. The swirling of air picked up napkins, cups, magazines, and even people.

Jim's mind immediately snapped into a fog and he lost his balance just as the door opened up. The incredible amount of drag that the jet produced gave a jerking motion to the left.

A loud, sudden bang shuttered the aircraft as the door continued to open further, being pulled into the airstream. The daylight continued to grow larger and larger, until the whole area was exposed to the outside.

The pressure difference was what experts would deem "explosive decompression." With the whole construction of the jet built through the eyes of safety, automated features began attempting to preserve life. The airplane's system recognized the pressure difference and deployed the oxygen masks.

The door extended about a couple inches before the wind grabbed hold of the stairs, pulling it farther from the fuselage. The wind snapped and bent the piano hinges, which were the only things keeping the door in place.

With everything going on and all non-secured objects flying out the door, Jim's eyes instantly gravitated towards Jenny's lifeless body, which was sliding along the floor, getting sucked closer and closer to the hole.

Jim reached out and swan dived for Jenny before the second large bang and shutter vibrated through the aircraft. With the door gone, nothing kept Jim or Jenny inside the aircraft. Jim's hand grasped Jenny's leg as his own legs snagged on the lip of the entrance.

Jim's sweaty hands couldn't hold on any longer to Jenny. The violent air rushed past the aircraft, pulling Jenny's body into the strong slipstream with ease.

With Jenny gone, Jim attempted to grasp something to pull himself back into the safety of the aircraft, but instead found James, whose arm was anchored to a seatbelt extender.

James reached over with his foot and started to kick Jim, until he, too, left the aircraft.

In the flight deck, the jet bounced and rolled violently. Mitch quickly grabbed the flight deck door and flung his arm until the air being sucked out of the gaping hole like a vacuum grabbed hold of the door and slammed it shut, the pressure differential keeping it securely against the bulkhead frame. The door had mechanically built-in decompression panels which allowed for less stress on the door while the pressure was allowed to equalize. The air started to equalize, giving Mitch the last couple seconds of useful consciousness to claw his way back to his seat and quickly threw on the oxygen mask.

As he reached around, he pulled the black nylon straps of his harness while using his other hand to try and stabilize the jet while keying up the radio at the same time.

"Mayday, mayday, mayday, Nor'easter Eleven Seventy-two, emergency descent to ten-thousand, explosive decompression!" Mitch announced over the radio, unable to hear any response.

The autopilot's disconnect alarm had continuously chirped since the initial upset, as the jet rolled uncommanded to the left. The sound of the wind that was hitting the windscreen was different. Mitch looked down and noticed the red and white over speed indicator, which was only present during excessive speed, which quickly crept down the airspeed indicator. This showed when the jet was accelerating and would over-speed and potentially over-stress.

All of Mitch's senses left him as his ears popped and his peaked stress sent him into shock. His mind was cloudy and his ears couldn't hear anything.

Mitch quickly latched onto the yoke, trying to right the aircraft while allowing the jet to maintain a controlled descent without ripping the wings off. He gently nursed the control back to the right, at least trying to get the wings level. Then he pulled on the yoke, trying to arrest the descent.

Slowly and gently, the nose started to rise and the wings leveled until the altimeter read 25,000 feet. The airspeed was bleeding off somehow, indicating that the plane was slowing down.

"Jesus fucking Christ!" Mitch yelled out, breathing heavily into his suffocating mask. His hair was caught in the harness for the mask, so every time he had to move his head, a sharp pinch of hair kept distracting him from his next task.

Mitch looked over to the right to his thrust levers as he grabbed both of them and yanked them to the idle position. The engines spooled down, which kept the jet from over-speeding.

Next to the thrust levers was the flight spoiler handle. He grabbed onto the lever with the meaty portion of his hand and yanked the handle to deploy any possible amount of drag that could stabilize the jet in a descent.

Within a few moments of the jet being in an upset condition, it started to stabilize. Mitch's mind was still in a fog, but he was slowly regaining his sense of hearing.

Mitch squeezed his eyes and shook his head again, trying to clear the brain fog. It took a couple seconds, but Mitch's ears finally picked up the continuously ringing bell that alerted crews of a fire, along with a computerized voice announcing, "Engine fire."

Fighting through the fog, Mitch glanced over his primary engine display, which was lit up like a red and yellow Christmas tree.

In the back of the cabin, all the passengers screamed at the top of their lungs, wrestling with the jungle of rubber hoses, which supplied them with the emergency air supply during a decompression event.

The cabin filled with heavy fog as the air within the cabin condensed into visible moisture.

Mitch hyper focused on the engine indications on the computer screen, his eyes naturally gravitating towards the red indication on the left (number one, the engine), which had caught fire.

Going back to his training, he remembered that there were very few things that would bring down a jet of that size.

Fire and acting hastily were two of them.

Being deliberate in his actions, Mitch continued to descend the jet while he reached up to the glare shield, where two square lights were flashing and shining directly into Mitch's eyes.

Distracted by the noise and lights, Mitch reached up and slapped both red and yellow buttons, extinguishing the lights and silencing the alarms.

Glancing over at the engine displays again, Mitch read the first red warning, "Engine fire."

Behind the flight deck door, James locked his hands together while gripping the seatbelt extender, which prevented him from getting sucked out of the gaping hole in the side of the airplane.

Losing consciousness, James gripped the seatbelt extender with one hand and reached out to grab one of the masks that was located by the flight attendant jump seat. He pulled the rubber hose, which pulled the pin on the chemical oxygen generator and activated the chemical reaction, producing breathable oxygen for him.

There was a severe scent of burning cloth, but it helped keep James' mental state somewhat present.

Back in the flight deck, Mitch kept telling himself, "Focus, just focus," as he was aware that stress caused crew to overlook the simplest things.

He slowed his process down. As he was the only pilot, he needed to double and triple check every switch and button he was touching.

"Okay, I have engine one on fire," Mitch said out loud, pointing his index finger at the display before moving his finger up and over to the glare shield, where another red square button was lit up vibrantly.

Mitch wrapped his longer fingers around the number one thrust lever, and pulled it back to the mechanical stop, making sure that he was being deliberate with his actions, remembering that doing the wrong things was, generally, worse than procrastination.

"Okay, Left Hand Engine Fire Push," Mitch read the label slowly and deliberately before he moved his finger back towards the display, confirming that it was indeed the left engine.

The button, when selected, began the shutdown sequence of the engine, turning off the fuel, electrical and hydraulic pumps, which allowed the engine to run.

Mitch lifted the clear plastic guard, which sat over the button, then pushed the red button, which illuminated a smaller green button just below it.

Waiting for a few moments for any indication of the fire dying off, Mitch then selected the green button, which discharged a halon fire-bottle directly into the left engine, starving the engine of oxygen and extinguishing the fire.

Confirming that he did not shut down the wrong engine, Mitch stared intently at the engine displays again, completely ignoring everything occurring on the other side of the flight deck door.

Grabbing the left thrust lever, Mitch brought it all the way back to the stops, making absolutely sure that he grabbed the left thrust lever and not the right, which controlled the operating engine. He lifted the small red toggle lever on the left thrust lever and pulled it to the shutoff position. This safety device prevented the thrust levers from inadvertently being shut-off in flight while the pilots pulled the handle all the way back.

Mitch pulled the thrust lever until it wouldn't go any further, and secured the dead engine.

On the other side of the flight deck door, in the cabin, passengers were looking around, fearing for their lives as the jet continued descending violently, being pushed around by the storms.

The outside was a milky grey as the jet descended through a thick cloud layer, the sunlight being diffused by trillions of tiny droplets.

As if the descent wasn't rough enough, the first-class passengers also still had perfect visibility of where James was hunkering down.

Back in the flight deck, once Mitch confirmed that he killed the dead engine and not the operating one, he glanced up at his displays. The jet was passing 22,000 feet, on its way down to a breathable altitude of 10,000 feet.

After forgetting for a moment that he was on oxygen, he reached up and looked at the overhead panel, where a white light was illuminated.

"Pass oxy," Mitch said to himself before it clicked, the oxygen masks deployed.

"Okay, that's good, I think we're stabilizing," Mitch said through his mask. "We're gonna be okay."

Back in the cabin, Wanda, who had been sitting back and nursing her facial wounds, got up from her seat and made sure that all the passengers were wearing masks. She tried to put the horror of what she had seen behind her, but her eyes couldn't fool any of the passengers.

"Pull the mask and put it on!" Wanda shouted as she stood up, demonstrating to the back half of the cabin on what to do. "It's just like we showed this morning. Pull the lanyard, which will start the flow of oxygen."

James finally got to his feet and shoved past the passengers as he made his way down the aisle to where Wanda was trying to regain some sort of control of her cabin.

"SIT THE FUCK DOWN!" James snarled over the extreme sound, instilling his dominance yet again.

The cabin was starting to get cold as all the heat was escaping from the hole, where the front passenger door once was.

Meanwhile, in the flight deck, Mitch rotated a couple knobs which allowed him to establish communications using the overhead speakers and the microphone in the oxygen mask, like he had practiced several times in simulated lessons. The only difference was that he had a counterpart in the flight deck to assist with making sure the wrong button wasn't pushed, or that the wrong lever wasn't pulled.

The remainder of the flight rested *entirely* on Mitch's shoulders, and he knew it.

"Center, Nor'easter Eleven Seventy-two, we are in a descent going down to ten-thousand feet. We have explosive decompression," Mitch said muffled through the mask, hoping to finally hear a response from the controller.

There was momentary silence over the radio. Mitch looked down to ensure that he configured the panel properly.

Finally, after a few seconds of radio silence, the radio chatter came to life.

Mitch continued with the descent. He looked at his display and his altitude read-out.

"Okay, 20,000 and going down," he thought to himself. He only had 13 minutes of passenger oxygen for the cabin, and he needed to be down and stable by that precise 13-minute mark.

Suddenly, the high-speed warning chirped from one of the displays. The red and white warning alerted the pilot that the jet was over speeding and risking severe damage.

Mitch gently and carefully rose the nose of the jet, arresting the descent a little bit as the jet continued to descend through 18,000 feet. He held the jet at that altitude, allowing the airspeed to bleed off and allow for another expeditious descent into the clouds, which didn't take much longer.

In the back, James was showing signs of hypoxia, his finger nailbeds and lips turning blue. He stumbled his way back to the front with his handgun in tow. He grabbed the oxygen mask and put it back on, taking several deep breaths before looking around again.

Around him, it was a scene of utter chaos, all the passengers in self-preservation mode. It was *exactly* what James wanted.

He noticed that no one was worried about him hijacking the airplane any longer. He could have done anything at this point, and hardly anyone would notice. His deranged mind began piecing together his next moves.

Chapter 8

Nor'easter 1172, In flight,
10,000 Feet Above Indianapolis
09:15 a.m.

Mitch leveled the jet at 10,000 feet and re-trimmed the control surfaces for a smoother flight, allowing for less force to keep the jet straight and level.

After a couple button pushes, he reached over to the autopilot control panel on the glare-shield of the jet and dialed in 10,000 feet and his current heading before pushing the autopilot connect button.

"Fuck you, Jim…" Mitch muttered to himself, completely disgusted with himself and the selfish actions of his new, inexperienced, first officer.

Not only did Jim not heed instructions by his boss, the captain, but he violated company and federal regulations to open the flight deck door during a hostage situation.

Mitch took a deep breath and pushed the button to engage the autopilot. With the autopilot engaged, Mitch looked over at the engine settings and pushed up on the thrust lever of the number two engine, on the right side, which allowed him to maintain the speed and altitude.

The jet responded favorably and started to regain its sense of control.

Satisfied with the current configuration of the aircraft, Mitch sat back and looked at all the warning messages that were displayed in front of him, trying to figure out which ones needed immediate responses versus what could wait until the jet was on the ground.

Starting with the red warnings first, Mitch pulled out his quick reference handbook and began flipping through the pages to the associated message and ran through the procedures before he actually began running the procedures to mitigate the warnings.

Normally, when there were two pilots, each pilot would double-check one another before they started to flip critical switches to ensure they didn't turn off their one good engine instead of securing a dead engine.

One by one, Mitch flipped switches until the autopilot disconnected unexpectedly again, which sounded the alarm, startling him.

Refocusing his eyes, Mitch looked around at the condition of the jet when the stall warning light flashed and the stick-shaker had activated. The pulsing of the yoke in his lap back and forth alerted Mitch of an impending stall.

Primacy came into play as Mitch quickly grabbed the yoke and pushed the controls forward, breaking the stall, and getting the jet flying again.

The jet lurched forward as the nose dropped, bringing the buckled passengers out of their seats, floating them inside the cabin, their stomachs feeling weightless as well.

Mitch's eyes automatically focused on the airspeed indicator and then on the engine thrust setting. He realized that his task saturation caused him to stall the airplane, which prevented the airplane from flying, as the wings were no longer able to produce the lift it needed to keep the jet aloft.

Understanding exactly what happened, Mitch shoved the one good thrust lever into the highest setting that could be produced, but the jet was still mushing and descending.

"What the fuck?!" Mitch yelled out, unsure of what exactly was happening. Something didn't feel right. The jet should have been able to fly on one engine just fine at that altitude. He couldn't figure out why the jet was slowing and unable to maintain altitude.

Mitch once again shoved the thrust lever, hoping it'd go just a little bit further, but it didn't. As he thrusted his arm against the thrust levers, his funny bone rubbed against the flight spoiler handle, sending an electric shock up his arm and into his shoulder.

"Fuck!" Mitch shouted, along with some other expletives that only he really understood.

Mitch looked down. His flight spoiler lever was still in the deployed position. He quickly shoved the lever forward, allowing a few more expletives to escape from his mind through his mouth.

The jet immediately began flying again. It jumped up abruptly and began flying smoothly again.

"Fucking Mitch, get your fucking shit together," Mitch said to himself, trying to mentally engage his brain versus just being strictly reactionary. He finally closed his eyes and looked down at the hose and wires connected to his face mask.

He grabbed the two paddles at the base of the mask, allowing the quick donning feature to release his head from the harness.

"Eleven Seventy-two."

Mitch snapped back to the present as a radio call interrupted his subconscious.

"Ah, Eleven Seventy-two, we are with you," Mitch replied.

Mitch could only hear the static from the radio and keyed the mic when he thought the center was done transmitting.

"Eleven Seventy-two, standby for a moment while I get my mask off," Mitch said, muffling through the mask.

Without too much of an issue, Mitch stowed the mask in its small case and reset the system, allowing for another use of emergency air if he absolutely needed to again.

Mitch took a deep breath and reset his primary headset over his ears as he pressed the push to talk button on the yoke and started his conversation with the controllers.

Mitch squeezed his eyes shut again, taking a moment to refocus on the situation at hand. Not entirely sure as to what happened, Mitch secured his headset over his ears again and repositioned his microphone over his mouth and keyed in.

"Ah, center, this is Eleven Seventy-two, we are level at ten-thousand," Mitch called out.

To his relief, the voice on the other end of the radio sprang to life as well.

"Roger, we are monitoring your situation here on radar and Dagger has been relaying information back. Please confirm your status," the air traffic controller asked over the unsecure airways.

"I-I don't know. Number one flight attendant was shot, the first officer opened the flight deck door. Now I'm all alone up here. The hijacker booby-trapped the main door with a rope and he opened it in inflight," Mitch called back.

"Mitch, this is Hainsworth, I'm off your left wing. We saw everything," Dagger Lead, the callsign of the fighter jets, called back with a somber voice.

"I- I think he got ejected too," Mitch hesitated for a moment, but then keyed up the mic again.

"The hijacker, I think he's gone," he said, not fully aware that the jet was still a hijacked jet, given the flight deck door was closed and secured again.

Another moment of silence filled the airwaves.

"We saw the first officer and a flight attendant get ejected. Only two individuals left the airplane," Hainsworth said.

"What else did you see?" Mitch asked Hainsworth.

"We watched the door open, all the way through the separation. We have GPS markings as to where those people left the aircraft and the local authorities are enroute to recover them along with the door."

Mitch's stomach, which had been tied in knots since earlier that morning, now tightened like it was being crushed by a vice.

"I-I was dating Jenny… I mean that flight attendant," Mitch said, trying to keep his voice strong, but it was involuntarily shaking.

"I'm sorry, Mitch," Hainsworth said.

"Sorry to interrupt, gentlemen, I've got Troy Higgins on frequency right now," Kevin, the controller announced.

"Captain?" Troy replied.

"Special Agent Higgins…" Mitch paused. "What can I do for you?"

"Captain, can you confirm what you just said? I need to make sure I have a clear mental photo as to what's going on up there," Troy replied.

Mitch sat back in his seat, reattaching and tightening his harness, securing himself to his seat. He took a deep breath and pressed the EMER CALL button on his audio control panel and waited. A few more seconds went by, but there was no response.

"Special Agent, I cannot get ahold of anyone in the back. As far as I am aware, we are still hijacked, as only two people were ejected from the airplane during the opening of the door," Mitch said.

"How many people are alive?" Troy asked in a calm yet matter-of-fact tone.

"I don't know," Mitch replied, emotionless and numb.

"What did you see when the door opened up?" Troy asked, trying to get Mitch to paint a mental picture.

"I-I saw some string or wire that was tied onto the ball-handle of the main entrance. He pulled the handle up and the wind and air took care of everything else," Mitch said as he looked out at the jets escorting the airliner.

Mitch's eyes caught the lead fighter's face. "Dagger, can you give me external updates? What can you see?" Mitch asked.

A slight chuckle came over the radio. "Where would you like me to start?" Hainsworth asked.

Mitch shook his head and keyed his microphone, "Okay, fair enough, from the front and we will work our way back to the tail-end of the airplane."

"Okay, Captain, let's start from the front. Your front door is missing. The piano hinges bent out into the airstream and the whole structure is just gone. You have nothing that you can do to plug the door," Hainsworth said.

"Okay," Mitch replied calmly, still feeling sick to his stomach over Jenny undoubtedly being dead. A heavy guilt weighted down his shoulders as his last memories of Jenny were ones of him being a jerk and not responding to her apologies or even listening to what she had to say.

Mitch turned his attention to the F-16 that had slowed slightly, allowing for a closer inspection of the leading edge of the wing.

"Okay, your leading edge and wing-root is damaged. I can see that there is venting of fuel from the wing. Looks like a puncture of sorts."

"Okay, hang on," Mitch called out on the radio.

Mitch looked at his displays. A yellow fuel imbalance alert was shown, along with a significantly lower left tank on the right. He looked up at the overhead panel.

"I won't need the gas in the left wing, so I'm just going to transfer it before we lose it," Mitch said as he selected the cross-feeding switches. The cross-feeding allowed as much fuel as possible to be switched from the damaged fuel tank to the one where he needed it.

Mitch looked at his iPhone and turned on a timer for a couple minutes.

"Okay, I'm back with you, Colonel," Mitch announced over the radio.

"Okay, let's continue…" Dagger One-One said, "You had an engine fire, the whole back is jet back. Did you use the bottle to extinguish it?"

Mitch looked at his displays and keyed the microphone.

"I did, do I need to use the second bottle?" Mitch asked.

"Maybe. I'd wait unless the conditions warrant," Dagger One-One replied as he moved the jet into position in the front left of the damaged jetliner and remained steady.

A few moments of silence was interrupted by Dagger One-One keying up the microphone.

"Ah, Captain, your hijacker is still onboard," the Colonel announced over the radio.

Mitch's hands turned cold and his heart skipped a beat at what was just transmitted over the radio.

"Wh-what? How can you tell?" Mitch stuttered.

A slight snicker made its way through the airwaves, the tall-tail sign of amazement, which came from the Colonel.

"Ah, he stuck his head out of the door and looked right at us. And… now, he's pointing a gun at us."

Just as the transmission concluded, Mitch ducked his head into his shoulders after the report of several gun shots were discharged at the fighter jet. One shot went off right after the other.

The reports continued as James continued to empty the magazine at an object that looked stationary.

James tossed out Richard's empty handgun and grabbed Mike's service weapon that was already loaded with a full magazine. He ducked back into the cabin, trying to keep control of the rest of the passengers.

"Col, get out of there!" Mitch screamed into the microphone. "Get in position behind us, and monitor there!"

The colonel yanked his jet to the left, broke off from the formation, and spun the jet around in a hard bank, disengaging from the hijacked jet.

After a few seconds of maneuvering, the F-16 ducked back and below, where James could see him from any vantage point.

James walked up to the flight deck door and slammed the meaty part of his hand on it several times. The loud noise spooked Mitch from his duties in trying to review the emergency procedures, initially causing him to drop his spiraled book of emergency procedures.

"Oh Captain, my captain!" James shouted. "Why are there fighter jets around us?!" James growled through the door.

"Because, some bastard hijacked my GODDAMN AIRPLANE!" Mitch shot back, turning his attention back to remedying the warnings and caution messages.

"Get them away, I don't want to see them again!" James yelled.

"I can't do anything about them. It's standard procedure for idiots who attempt to take over airplanes!" Mitch said, thinking of ways to keep the fighters around and use them to his advantage.

James paused for a moment on the other side of the flight deck door, "Okay, well, have them watch this, then…"

Mitch keyed the microphone, "Dagger, he's trying something, can you see what he's trying to do?"

"I'm on it," the Colonel said as he pushed and pulled the jet back into a vantage point to see the front passenger door, just to the left of the left wing, and below.

Mitch sat in his seat, in silence for what felt like an eternity.

"Colonel?" Mitch finally spoke up on frequency.

In the back of the cabin, the loud rush of air continued to disrupt the reality that the passengers were faced with. Many faces were blank, and others were of horror as James walked back towards the rear of the aircraft, where his original seat was, and where this entire ordeal started.

Looking around at the dead bodies that littered the whole aft portion of the jet, James grabbed one of the detention officers, whose body hadn't moved since the initial attack, and started dragging him feet first towards the front of the aircraft, sliding him down the aisle.

Gasps from the onlooking passengers were barely audible, but still enough to catch James' attention.

James stopped and looked around, his eyes narrowing. Looking like he was trying to spook a little child during bedtime ghost stories, he waved his gun in the air again, like he had to make political points.

"Keep your fucking heads down," James snarled at the passengers in close proximity. The back of his neck was very red, as if he knew that people were watching his every move.

James grabbed Robert by the legs again and dragged his lifeless body down the aisle and to the front door, where he laid the body down right next to where the main exit had been previously. James then motioned Wanda to come over to where he had been holding his position.

Wanda was extremely hesitant, but the fear of getting shot like Jenny made her overcome it.

"Call the captain on this phone," James shouted through the ambient noise of the air burbling against the open hole in the side of the jet.

Wanda's hands were trembling, her fingers stiff as a wet noodle. She couldn't find the fine motor skills that she needed in order to press the appropriate button. It wasn't until she hyper focused her eyes and deliberately pushed the flight deck call button with every muscle fiber tensing up.

"Yes?" Mitch answered in a sort of cold, matter-of-fact tone.

"Captain, it's Wanda, he wants to talk with you," Wanda said with pain in her stomach. She hadn't realized that her stomach and core muscles hadn't relaxed since the initial hijacking. Her muscles were so tense that she couldn't breathe. It was a truly horrific feeling, not being able to properly breathe.

Finally, after forcing her muscles to relax slightly, she began taking in full deep breaths which cleared her mind a little better than it had. She stood motionless, her feet feeling the engine vibration and the buffets from the wind, kicking around the smaller jet.

Wanda finally turned and looked at James again. Several moments passed, and James had moved from the galley and was standing at the sharp edge of where the door once was, with Richard's dead body halfway hanging off the ledge.

"What are you doing?!" Wanda shouted at James hysterically.

James stuck his head out of the gaping hole and glanced over where the lead F-16 had been. He couldn't see the other one, but figured it was somewhere out there.

"Goodbye, Dick," James said in a highly sarcastic tone as he shoved Richard's dead body out of the door, his arms and legs flopping in the wind.

The F-16 that was flying just above and to the left rear of the CRJ got a full view of his body. The engine blocked most of the passenger window view, but it was still a clear line of sight from the front passenger door.

"Oh my God," the Colonel replied, watching as a flailing dead body was brought up to the door, sat up in an upright, slouched position before it was kicked out of the door. The impact of the motionless body was violent as it struck the wing before the wind dragged the body under the jet and out of view.

The second F-16, the Colonel's wingman, which was sitting in a modified overwatch position to the rear of the CRJ and below the centerline, had seen a black object leave the aircraft, with a trajectory towards the wingman at a high closure rate.

"Two breaking off!" the second fighter jet announced tensely over the radio as the pilot spun the jet off to the right.

"What a sick idiot!" the second pilot shouted through the radio, disregarding his military bearing and courtesies when using the radio.

Richard's dead body twisted and rolled, being buffeted in the wind as it disappeared quickly into the lower cloud layer.

A couple moments later, after the two fighter jocks sat in silence after the first jettison, another person appeared in the aircraft doorway of the jet.

"Oh my God!" the second fighter announced over the radio, "are these already dead or are they willfully jumping?" the second fighter asked.

"Two, this is one, I think they're already gone. This is so gut-wrenching and so wrong. I have no words on what I'm seeing," Colonel said somberly. The physical pain of watching the horror was too much to be expressed through a microphone and transmitted through the air.

In the flight deck, Mitch sat quietly, listening to the radio calls between his two escorts as they were remarking at the inhumane act that was occurring right in front of them, on the other side of the flight deck door.

Going through the checklists, Mitch finally reached the last item that displayed on his warning screen. The item required no interaction, so he just let it go.

Mitch set the quick reference handbook down and rubbed his eyes quickly. The pages that he needed were neatly opened up along with a sheet of paper of pages that he would need in order to calculate the landing performance data.

"Eleven Seventy-two, you still with us?" the center controller asked, realizing that there hadn't been a lot of conversation with the hijacked jet for a little bit of time.

Mitch closed his eyes briefly and squeezed. He was trying to refocus his eyes with all the problems at hand, which just weren't getting any better. Jenny's face kept creeping into his head, his jet was highly damaged, his first officer martyred himself, and on top of that, the jet was still hijacked.

"Wait, Jenny," Mitch sighed softly as his mind wandered a bit.

Her lovely face and their passionate love before they came to work. Her lovely, scrunched face that she made when Mitch told another one of his typical "dad jokes."

Long lost mental pictures of Jenny were quickly replaced with her final moments onboard the aircraft... *his* aircraft. Her motionless body laying on the door haunted Mitch.

"Why are things so complicated and lonely?" Mitch asked himself, fully expecting his own mind to come up with a legitimate answer.

Mitch again momentarily flashed back to his time in Afghanistan. He was being shaken by the medics who were trying to work on his motionless friend, who laid on the ground motionless after a rocket landed right next to them.

Mitch's attention was jostled to the present again by the sound of another couple bangs onto the flight deck door. The longer-term mental alertness was obviously draining Mitch.

"What the fuck?!" Mitch shouted out, jolted from his daydream.

"That must have been a great show, the jets are nowhere to be found," James said jokingly as he placed his hand and cupped it to the door, attempting to listen for any sort of conversation regarding himself.

"Go ahead, jump off the ledge!" Mitch shouted as he shook his head at what he was hearing on the other side of the flight deck door.

"Now, get us on the ground before I start tossing out more people. Live people, this time," James said lightly, trying to make his point stick that he didn't have a care in the world.

Chapter 9
Nor'easter 1172, In flight,
09:25 a.m.

Mitch reached over to the middle of the center panel, the one that sat between the pilot and co-pilot, after James threatened more lives would be lost if he did not comply with the requirement to land the jet.

His hands covered his eyes as the pressure of being a captain of his jet, and now the most gut-wrenching feeling of being responsible for the deaths of his own passengers, was getting too unbearable.

"Nor'easter Eleven Seventy-two, suggest a heading of three-five-zero, deviation for weather," the controllers' voice popped into Mitch's radio, which turned his attention away from his sorrows.

Mitch sniffled before he keyed up the microphone, "Roger, over to three five zero."

He reached up to the flight control panel and dialed in a new heading into the autopilot system as the plane began turning. Just as his workload continued to increase, Mitch looked out the window at the milky grey imagery outside.

"And Eleven Seventy-two, are you able to climb at all?" the controller asked.

"I can, maybe to twelve? Would that help?" Mitch replied, looking at his instrument panel and assessing the maximum pressure for his passengers.

"Could you climb and maintain twelve-thousand on that heading?" the controller asked, hesitant to even suggest such a thing, especially with an exposed cabin.

"You got it," Mitch replied as he dialed the new altitude and increased the thrust, allowing the jet to climb slowly and gently.

Suddenly, as the jet rose a thousand feet, there was another sound of a beating fist pounding against the door. James was loudly expressing his agitated state.

Frustrated that he was being ignored, James stormed to the back of the jet, close to where he found a little girl and her mother.

James grabbed the little girl, but her mother protested out of anger and extreme fear. The little girl was a beautiful 2-year old who really didn't understand what was going on, but sensed the anger and tension of what was going on within the jet.

"Maddie, oh please God, no!" the girl's mother shouted grief-strickenly, her face streaming with tears.

The passengers nervously looked back at the commotion.

The man from seat 13B stood up. His hands were in front of him, his palms facing out.

"This is enough," the man said, trying to be firm with James.

"Shuddup," James slurred.

"No, enough."

James looked at the slightly oversized man approaching him and the young girl. With each step the man took, James' blood began to boil until he couldn't take the tense situation any further.

James rose his gun from the girl's shoulder and leveled the barrel towards the man blocking the aisle.

"Let her go!" the man said definitively, again trying to dissolve the situation, despite having a gun aimed at him.

"SIT DOWN!" James shouted as he pulled the trigger, causing the gun to spit out hot lead.

The bullet moved quicker than a blink of an eye, and had tracked for the man's center of mass, despite the moderate turbulence.

The man's left shoulder flew backwards, tossing him right into his seat. He let out an awful yell as he grabbed his bleeding shoulder.

With the commotion focused around the man from 13B, another much older man rose from his seat. His eyes glared at James as if he was looking for a fight, his frail arms and legs standing tall.

"Let her go!" the elderly man shouted at the top of his lungs, making sure his voice sounded as menacing as his battle-hardened eyes.

"Sit down, old man!" James shouted back, matching the volume of the man.

James' blood pressure began skyrocketing again, after being faced with another man trying to challenge his authority.

The old man's wife tugged at his tan windbreaker jacket as she spoke semi-audibly, "Sit down, Arnold. Sit down!"

Arnold looked down at his wife, calming her with a motion of his hand on her shoulder, "It's okay, my dear."

Arnold was an old World War II veteran, and his black hat was embroidered with the words "WORLD WAR II," along with the dates and the word "VETERAN." He wore the hat proudly, along with his medal suspended by a rainbow-colored ribbon, uniquely identified as the Légion d'honneur, given to those service members who endured the bloodbath of the Normandy invasion in Europe.

"Sit down, old man," James snarled again, running short on patience.

"You let her go, and then I'll sit down," Arnold replied.

James pointed the gun right at Arnold's face, the turbulence getting more pronounced to be accurate with the handgun.

"You either sit down or I blow your old decaying brain all over the people in front of you," James shouted, as he started moving towards the forward galley.

Arnold clenched his lips together and glared at James for a moment, staring down the madman who had been mentally torturing the passengers.

"You think this is the first time someone's pointed a gun in my face? I've been through worse, and I'm not going to let evil win. Let her go and I'll sit down with my wife."

Arnold motioned at the little girl, who was trying to weasel out of James' overly large hands.

James stood there for a minute and then looked down at the little girl, Maddie. She was young, gorgeous, and cute. The flickering of the sun bouncing between clouds vibrantly illuminated the light brown streaks in her dark brown hair. Her eyes were wide, signaling fear of what was about to unfold, but her cheeks were red, with large crocodile tears rolling down them.

James turned around to look at the girl's mother, who continued to protest and also had tears rolling down her face uncontrollably.

As he looked back towards the forward exit, a dark shadow overcame James' eyesight when a smaller red cylinder came into view and cracked him straight across his right eye.

James staggered back, releasing his death grip on little Maddie, who immediately fell to the floor and ran to her mother's arms, crying and shaking.

James grabbed his face, checking for obvious signs of blood.

Confident that he hadn't seen any blood or other trauma, James caught a glimpse of a couple adults encroaching in his space. His eyes were somewhat fuzzy and seeing stars after the strike.

With only a split second to look up, it didn't take long until a robust fight started occurring in the back of the airplane. James fell to the ground after being overpowered by the small group of angry men.

While being rushed, James discharged the gun three times, aimed at various locations, in hopes that he would have been able to injure at least one of his attackers, but the turbulence didn't allow for an accurate shot placement.

A mass of three large adults came over James as he regained some clarity. A bald man, Donnie, stood over James with a smaller halon fire extinguisher in hand.

Donnie sat in the aisle seat a few rows before Maddie and her mother, right below the overhead compartment where the fire extinguisher was stowed.

Donnie grabbed James' firearm in an attempt to gain control of him.

"Fuck, that gun is hot!" Donnie shouted, as he gripped the barrel of the gun.

As Donnie did his part, another man, a heavier set gentleman in a suit, followed up behind him, lending his assistance to secure James.

"Fuck you!" James shouted, as his arms were being pinned to the ground.

"Stop fighting it," Donnie commanded.

The scene was eerily reminiscent of the post 9/11 incident where a Muslim passenger was subdued and died after anxious passengers suffocated him for praying onboard the jet.

Donnie grabbed the gun again after readjusting his grip on the rack, pushing and putting the gun out of battery so the gun wouldn't discharge.

Donnie wrestled with James, who was kicking his legs around, trying to subdue his attacker as well as the heavier set bystander who charged up from the back of the airplane.

While kicking violently, James' feet caught the bystanders' ankle, causing him to lose balance with the flailing. Along with the progressively worse turbulence, things in the cabin began bouncing more and more violently as the jet passed another storm cell.

The bystander fell on top of Donnie, whose foot got caught under one of the seat braces.

An audible snap was heard as the heavier bystander's body got tangled up with Donnie. Donnie's tibia and fibula failed under the extreme weight of the bystander.

"No!" Donnie yelled, who was the only saving grace in controlling both the gun and James at the same time.

With his loud yelp of pain, Donnie released his death grip on James' gun, which put the gun back in battery and was capable of discharging again.

James pulled his arm back, positioned the gun so the grip rested on his chest, and pulled the trigger once again.

The gun barked loudly but the slide shot back, jabbing James right in the chest, causing a mis-feed of the gun.

The gun lobbed the hot projectile at several hundred feet per second and embedded inside Donnie's upper left chest, which instantly disabled him.

The gunshot wound instantly caused Donnie to drop flat, face-first, allowing James to get back up and regain his situational awareness, despite being hit in the head with a fire extinguisher.

While getting back up, the second bystander grabbed the halon bottle from Donnie, aimed it at James, and discharged some of the contents into the air, causing a white fog to fill the cabin.

James swung the gun around towards the bystander, who had his hands up and was backing up at the same time. Not wasting any time, James pulled the trigger again, its reverberations echoing throughout the cabin.

Unsatisfied with the result, James reached over and grabbed the small fire extinguisher, swinging it violently at whomever was in the way while he grabbed the rack of the gun and re-racked a round back into the chamber.

There was immense fear in the bystander's eyes, as he was sure that this was his last defining act as a failure to stop a hijacking, simply because he tripped.

James reached up with his free hand, feeling his cheek and right eye, which he couldn't see out of.

"Jesus fucking Christ!" James shouted as he brought the gun up, its barrel level with the bystander.

"Please don't!" the bystander pleaded.

"Shouldn't have intervened. You would have lived longer. Come over here, and bring your buddy with," James said with a slight smile.

The bystander grabbed Donnie, who had been lying motionless on the aisle floor, and put Donnie's body over his shoulder, and was ushered to the front of the plane by James, who was following from behind Donnie and the bystander.

"Okay, now toss him out," James said nonchalantly.

"Wh-what?" the bystander asked, not mentally comprehending what was being asked of him.

"Toss him out," James replied again, this time gesturing the gun towards the open door.

"I-I can't do that," the bystander replied.

"Shame," James replied shaking his head as he pulled the trigger, popping off one more round, and then another, forcing Donnie and the bystander to leave the aircraft in such a way that there would have been no recovery or anything to grab onto, leaving them to fall to the earth below.

There were audible gasps of horror and disbelief from the seats behind first class as the muffled sound of a thud hit the leading edge of the jet's wing.

Satisfied that the rest of the passengers wouldn't try to retake the plane, James ejected the empty magazine and slapped a full 15-round magazine into the gun and racked the slide shut, readying it for the next encounter.

As James walked over to the front door, he looked out of the hole at the increasing layer of clouds firming up. He couldn't see the ground any longer. The threatening thunderstorms to the left and the right of the airplane told the tail of why the air was beginning to become more and more turbulent.

Flashes of lightning impressively climbed the tall anvil-shaped clouds that surrounded the jet. James watched the whole event until the plane became surrounded by a thick dark cloud.

The turbulence quickly became more pronounced, but manageable until an air pocket dropped the floor right out from James.

With the lack of something solid to anchor his feet on, coupled with the suction of the wind pulling all the pressurized air from the pressurization system, James was pulled slowly towards the passenger door. He flailed his hands and arms around, attempting to grab ahold of something more solid, in hopes of pulling himself back to safety.

As James continued to slide uncontrollably through the door, his eyes locked onto one of the passengers sitting in the window seat in the first row. The man tried getting to his feet, but was tossed back by the turbulence. The attempt to get the plane rid of its hijacker was hardly achievable with the violent buffeting and tossing that the plane was experiencing.

Finally, as James neared the hole where the door was once held secure, he grabbed ahold of the small lips that were the securing mechanism of the passenger service door.

The cold wind grabbed James' legs and swiftly pulled him out into the airstream of the jet. The wind was extremely intense, whipping the fabric of James' pants around his legs, almost like a flag blowing in hurricane winds.

It took several moments and exhaustive effort to pull himself back into the cabin. Slowly, James flexed his muscles and somehow defied gravity, along with the impeding wind.

Once James exited the airstream, he fell right to the floor of the entryway to catch his breath.

In the flight deck, Mitch watched out of the side windows at the lightning before keying up the microphone.

"Center, Eleven Seventy-two, do you have any idea if there is a gap for us between this weather?" Mitch asked.

"Negative, you're going through the thinnest part of the weather, are you using your weather radar?" the controller replied.

A few more moments of silence oozed through the radio, and then the radio came back to life.

"Mitch, this is Kevin, your controller. I have an FBI negotiator tied into the center. He wants to speak with you," Kevin said.

"Alright," Mitch replied.

"Hi Mitch, it's Special Agent Troy Higgins. I have some information for you, but first, we want to confirm a few different things with you," Troy said over the radio.

"Sure, Troy, I'm all ears," Mitch said as he dialed back his speed to capture his new altitude.

"Okay, so, first off, are you alone in the flight deck?" Troy asked.

"I am," Mitch replied confidently.

"Is there a way we can speak with him, or them?" Troy asked.

Mitch looked puzzled and keyed the microphone, "Not unless I let him into the flight deck, and I'm not going to do that."

"Okay. I understand that the hijacker was the prisoner transfer that was onboard your aircraft. Is that correct?" Troy asked.

"I believe so. Everything happened so fast," Mitch replied.

"Okay, is there anyone else who is in control of the situation besides yourself and your hostage taker?" Troy asked for his third question.

Mitch sat back in his seat, thinking about the question posed. There was one hijacker, why did Troy ask about him and the hijacker?

"Ah, Troy, why are you worried about me? I'm not the one who hijacked the jet," Mitch countered.

"I understand that, but you are the one flying the jet, and not allowing me to talk to the real hijacker, so I have to cover my bases," Troy replied.

"It sure sounds like you're considering me a suspect, too," Mitch replied annoyed.

"Look, Mitch, we need to make sure that there are no other threats. You're in control of the jet, so logically you call for a hijacking and you're unwilling to let us communicate through the hijacker directly. What are we supposed to think?" Troy asked.

"How about you knock off the 20-question game and let me know your thoughts on this situation?" Mitch snarled back. "I want to land this Goddamn airplane so you can fuck this guy up."

"I understand. We are trying to get a picture as to how many people are onboard the aircraft that could be considered hostile. This will gauge our response," Troy said calmly.

"I only saw one guy in the back with a gun. That's all I saw!" Mitch yelled through the microphone, elevating his level of frustration.

"Okay," Troy conceded, sensing that the conversation couldn't go anywhere but worse from here. "We will plan on one hostile, but expect for you to be detained. You, along with all the other passengers, once you get the jet on the ground. You are about 20 minutes from landing, so we will be waiting for you. Roll out to the very end of the runway, and we'll be there," Troy said, conveying the plan over the radio, but not trying to give away too many details.

"I hope you brought a ladder," Mitch replied somewhat jokingly.

"We have a couple of them," Troy laughed.

"We will likely have our passengers put their heads down, in a brace position," Mitch added cautiously, since he knew that there was a good chance that his hijacker might overhear the plan. "Most of the passengers should comply with the brace position, but there are some that likely won't, so you'll have about 15 seconds after the jet stops rolling to get onboard and take over the situation."

"Understood. We'll be ready for you, Captain," Troy replied.

Mitch sat back in his seat again. Something didn't quite feel right about the whole encounter.

"Why haven't they asked if we had any demands?" Mitch asked out loud, querying the universe.

Mitch leaned forward towards the yoke and glanced out of the window. The fighter aircraft, which had been flying in formation with the CRJ, were now gone, likely to a position five miles behind, covertly escorting him.

Mitch reached over to the intercom panel and keyed up the flight attendant station. The phone was almost immediately picked up by James.

"What are your intentions?" Mitch asked in a monotone voice.

"You know my one intention, get me on the ground," James replied.

"Other than that, the FBI wants to know what to expect from you," Mitch asked, poking a little bit more.

"Either you get me on the ground or I'll force this jet down," James replied.

Mitch had a cold shiver run up and down his spine. He managed to get out, "Oh, and how do you plan on doing that? You took out the one door that could have been opened in flight."

"You don't really know much about me, do you?" James replied.

"Ask me on the ground if I really care," Mitch replied, poking the bear a little bit more.

"You only have one engine left, and we're unpressurized. It's not going to take a lot for me to open an over-wing exit and toss the 50 pounds of metal down the throat of the engine," James threatened.

"In fact, hang on for a moment," James said, then disconnected the intercom.

Mitch pressed a soft key on the display panel, which brought up the synoptic display of all the doors.

"What are you doing?" Mitch queried himself as he called up Troy again in St. Louis.

"Troy, he's going to try and bring us down. I don't know if he can, but he's going to try pulling another door and chucking it into the engine," Mitch announced over the radio.

A couple seconds ticked by before any sort of response came across the airwaves. Mitch keyed the microphone again, "Troy, why haven't you guys asked about demands yet? Can we try some diplomacy to at least get us to some good weather airports?"

A sound of exhaling air through the radio peaked Mitch's ears.

"There is no negotiation with terrorists."

Mitch sat in his seat stunned. "Are you guys going to force us down?" he asked.

"Stay away from populated areas. If you don't, then yes, we will force you down," Troy replied somewhat suppressed, making sure that his voice carried the meaning that he wanted it to.

"Wait, what?" Mitch shot back, shocked.

Mitch's mouth suddenly became dry as his mind shuffled through the various possibilities. Surely the military wasn't going to shoot down an airliner *full* of innocent passengers and a single crazy guy?

Onboard Dagger One-One, Colonel Hainsworth finished his conversation and confirmation of orders from Washington. He looked over at his wingman, who was trailing to the right.

"Two, you understand your orders?" Hainsworth asked.

"Affirmative," Hainsworth's wingman replied.

Chapter 10
Dagger One-One

Hainsworth looked once again at his wingman as a lump welted up in his throat. He looked down at his radar scope, and confirmed the present location in reference to the last moments he would have to make the decision of launching one of his weapons against a hijacked civilian aircraft.

"Eleven Seventy-two, this is Dagger One-One, suggest a turn to the right sixty degrees," Hainsworth said.

Mitch was slow to respond, puzzled with the suggestion, but banked the aircraft as instructed.

"What's the game plan?" Mitch asked.

"We need to keep you away from populated areas," Hainsworth replied in a mono-tone voice.

The radio fell silent again for a moment before Mitch came back over the radio. "You guys are behind us now, aren't you? Lining up a shot," he said.

Hainsworth's head dropped. Feelings of guilt crept into his mind; not only did he sacrifice this guy's dream for becoming a fighter pilot because he didn't "like" what he looked like, but now, in an ironic twist of fate, he would have to shoot down this guy's airliner.

"We are just told to keep you away from populated areas. If the hijacker gains access to the aircraft, then yes, we need to take you guys down," Hainsworth said, knowing full well that was a small white lie.

Onboard Flight 1172
09:35 a.m.

James' brain was processing information rather quickly as he walked past the seat where the deceased husband had been, in seat 6A, before he was tossed out of the airplane.

He was supposed to be an air marshal. Something didn't feel right. He stood and glanced at the seat where the dead husband sat for a couple of long seconds.

His mind was racing over the past several hours. Something didn't sit well with him.

James started questioning the two seats where the Air Marshals were supposed to be sitting.

"6A was supposed to be an Air Marshal, but it wasn't. He had a ticket for 13B," James muttered to himself. "There was nobody in 13A, which was supposed to be the Air Marshal, but nobody was there."

James looked back at seat 6A again and mumbled, "If the guy moved from 13B to 6A, then 13B should be empty, but it's not."

Finally, the hair on the back of James' neck stood up and his eyes got large.

"Fuck, there *is* an air marshal onboard," he muttered somewhat audibly as he twisted his head around, scanning the rows of seats behind him.

"What was that fucking seat?" James asked himself as he started making his way down the aisle full of hysterical passengers.

"13A, but it was empty. 13B had a guy in it. If the guy in 6A had a ticket for 13B, then the guy in 13A moved to 13B," he concluded.

"That's gotta be the marshal!" James rationalized as he walked down the aisle, suddenly making eye contact with the *real* air marshal.

The air marshal's face turned pale white as he realized that he was made. He already had a gunshot wound to his left shoulder, but fortunately enough, his dominant right hand was left unharmed.

The marshal conspicuously snuck his hand into the seat's back pocket and grabbed his service weapon, which had been hiding since the beginning of the trip.

Realizing that he was at a clear disadvantage, the marshal got to his feet and scooted back several rows, trying to gain a larger picture of what was playing out in front of him. It was also an attempt to distance himself from the action between Wanda and James.

James had risen his gun towards the marshal. All his focus was brought on by the one adversary, when Wanda came up behind him with a seatbelt extender in hand.

With a shaking pair of hands, she a whipped the belt around James' neck in one fluid motion and snagged the opposite end with her free hand and clipped the seatbelt extender to itself. The motion was almost like Wanda had practiced this technique before.

James, caught off-guard by the new attack, attempted to fight back, but not before Wanda was able to grab ahold of the loose end and pulled as tight as she could, cinching the belt tightly against James' neck.

The marshal stuck his gun between his knees and squeezed them together and shoved down, shoving the slide to the rear position, before loosening his legs and allowing the slide to close. The motion was less than ideal, but with James slowed down, chambering a round this way was more than feasible. With a round now chambered, the marshal leveled the barrel towards James, who was still struggling with Wanda.

Using a technique in college wrestling, James tossed Wanda over his shoulder, causing her to land face-first into the head rest, blocking the clear shot that the marshal had of James.

James bent over, reached for the buckle flap and released the buckle, allowing him to take in a deep breath.

James, still disoriented and caught off guard at the attempted retaking of the aircraft, rose his gun in the rough direction of the marshal and pulled the trigger a couple times while still trying to fight off Wanda, who had a death grip on the detached end of the seatbelt extender.

Wanda flung the metal-tipped strap around like she was trying to tame a pit full of venomous snakes, striking James several times in his face and cheek.

James' face turned beet red as he trained his handgun back towards Wanda, who was doing a good job of staying away from the business end of the gun.

The air marshal took a couple more steps back and leveled his gun's sights on James, adrenaline pulsing through his veins. He struggled to get a clear shot at James without risking injury to Wanda.

"Wanda, get down!" the marshal shouted, hoping that she heard his command.

Wanda glanced over at the marshal, and without even thinking, released James from her death grip. He went flying backwards a few feet as his weight and center of gravity shifted, instantly shedding the extra 90 pounds of Wanda hanging off him.

Finally, a clear shot came into view when James got to his feet, and the marshal pulled the trigger. The thunderous report of the gun's report shook the immediate area, and the slide shot back with the explosive force, ejecting the bullet casing into the air.

The bullet left the barrel at a bone-crushing speed and embedded in James' chest. He didn't go down easily, for the round had chewed up everything in its path before it struck him. He staggered backwards towards the main door of the aircraft. His face mimicked someone who was in shock, and couldn't feel a thing.

As James was staggering towards the front of the airplane, the marshal took another two shots, employing the rifleman theory of two rounds in the center mass, and one kill shot in the head.

After the rounds found their accurate target, the taller gentleman sitting in seat 1B grabbed James by the collar and used his momentum to eject him out of the gaping hole, where the exit door once was.

James' body disappeared from sight before striking the leading edge of the wing, causing a soft thud to be heard inside the cabin.

Everyone's ears within the cabin rang from the louder and heavier gunshot that the marshal had carried.

Wanda took a minute before she got to her feet, not fully comprehending what she saw. Before long, she snapped back from this daze by the sight of a nice, heavier set passenger trying to lift her up from the ground.

The cabin was still loud with wind, but the overbearing whimpering and crying of the passengers, finally being able to breathe, overtook the volume of the wind, making the sounds audible across the entire cabin.

Wanda scanned the cabin again to ensure that there were no more surprises. Realizing that there had been armed escort fighters previously, she raced over to the intercom, where she fumbled through the whole process of dialing the flight deck.

"Flight deck," Mitch called, somewhat stressed with his heavy workload, trying to ensure that he didn't give away that they were likely not going to make it back to any airport.

A noise broke through the static. "James is dead! He's gone!" Wanda yelled through the interphone system.

Mitch sat silently, trying to comprehend what Wanda just told him.

"What, how?" Mitch asked, shocked.

"Another guy with a gun, he shot him," Wanda replied excitedly, but out of breath as her mind swirled at the possibility of another turn of fate.

"What? Where did this guy come from? A good guy?" Mitch asked, his mind racing through all the other possibilities.

"I-I think it's a cop. I had a feeling about this guy. I think he's an air marshal," Wanda finally blurted out.

Mitch, still concerned, tried to mentally process what Wanda just told him. Focusing on the huge mountain ahead of him, Mitch disconnected the phone and wrapped his hands around the quick reference handbook, trying to manually calculate the performance numbers for a safe landing.

A few seconds passed as Mitch turned the jet back towards St. Louis, and his fighter escort followed suit.

Mitch continued looking through the calculations and paperwork, but then realized that the ones who needed to know were the *last* to know.

He frantically keyed up the microphone and broadcasted across the network, "Our hijacker is dead!"

Mitch held his breath for a moment, hoping to get some sort of reply from any of the listeners.

"Nor'easter Eleven Seventy-two is under control," Mitch announced again. "Dagger One-One?"

A tingling sensation of worry crept into his mind. "Why is nobody answering me?" Mitch asked out loud.

"Center, Eleven Seventy-two, can I get direct to St. Louis?"

"Standby," the center controller replied.

A single "ding" echoed through the flight deck. Instinctively, Mitch looked at one of the engine displays and, which also gave an indication of anything wrong with the airplane. There, he found a yellow "ICE" was illuminated on the screen.

"Fuck, what else can go wrong?!" Mitch snarled to himself as he reached to the overhead panel and turned on the wing and cowl anti-ice, which allowed hot air to be tapped off the engines to rid the airplane of ice, allowing the jet to fly more efficiently and safely.

Mitch looked out the side window, trying to locate any of the fighter jets.

"Colonel Hainsworth, we are no longer a threat, you can come and join us," Mitch announced.

Another bout of doubt crept into Mitch's mind. The fighters were a couple miles behind them, and they were also carrying live weapons.

Suddenly, his hair stood up on end. "They're going to shoot us down!" Mitch thought to himself.

"Colonel, there is no need to shoot us down. Our hijacker is dead!" Mitch announced again, as he pointed the jet right towards St. Louis' airport.

Mitch's palms began to get sweaty again. He looked out and the outskirts of the city limits were just coming into view.

"If they're going to shoot us down, it'll be now or never," Mitch thought to himself.

Mitch's attention was drawn away by an alert inside the flight deck. After the anti-ice switches were flipped, a triple ding (chime sound) echoed through the flight deck, accompanied by an aural warning, "Smoke, Smoke, Smoke."

Mitch looked at his glass display once again and noticed that the forward cargo bay, under the cabin floor, was indicating a fire. Quickly thinking, Mitch reached over to the aft portion of the center pedestal, where two red-guarded buttons were located. The guards were there as a safety precaution to ensure that the wrong button wasn't pushed by accident. One of the buttons was lit up red.

Mitch's heart skipped a beat as he flipped the protective cover and pressed the button, which illuminated a green discharge light for the fire suppression system to be activated.

Just before he selected the green button, the second red light illuminated, indicating a fire in the aft cargo compartment, which was located in the tail of the airplane, behind the bathrooms in in the back.

"You have GOT to be fucking kidding me!" Mitch shouted out loud, in the empty cockpit. "What are the fucking chances for a fire in *both* cargo compartments?"

Mitch removed his hand from the fire panel and looked at his display.

"The ducting must have been damaged when the passenger door left the aircraft and struck the wing?" Mitch asked himself.

"Fuck it," Mitch proclaimed, reaching over and selecting the belly cargo compartment as the option to discharge the halon agent.

"Approach, Eleven Seventy-two, I have to step away, I have a fire indication in both cargo bays," Mitch said calmly over the radio.

Not hearing any response from the controllers or the fighter jets behind him, Mitch released the harness and got out of his captain's seat. His left eye still stung from when Jim decked him.

He reached behind the empty first officer's seat and retrieved the one and only weapon that the crew had onboard the aircraft, the crash axe. He also reached for the halon fire extinguisher from behind his seat, first checking the peep hole to verify that nothing was going on.

Looking at the overhead panel, Mitch then ducked under the overhead panel and deselected the anti-ice system switches. Then he cautiously unlatched the flight deck door and opened it, meeting Wanda face to face, along with the air marshal's.

"Captain?!" Wanda shouted.

Mitch pulled Wanda and gently shoved her into the seat. "Sit in Jim's seat," Mitch said.

"What the fuck is going on now?" Wanda asked worriedly.

Mitch turned and was face to face with the armed air marshal, "who the fuck are you?" Mitch said, short on patience.

Wanda turned around, "That's the air marshal, he's a good guy." Wanda said with a stunned look on her face, "what's going on?"

"No time to explain, reach out and find if there is a passenger with flying experience," Mitch said as he turned towards the air marshal.

"Anyone other than myself trying to get into the flight deck, you shoot them!" Mitch told him as he left the flight deck.

The marshal looked at Mitch with a sign of confusion, but the aural warnings, "Smoke... smoke" connected the dots as to what was happening.

As Mitch made his way through the cabin towards the rear lavatory, the looks on all the passengers' faces were still ones of complete terror.

After all they had been through, they didn't know what to expect. If this flight wasn't horrific enough, now, a guy in a pilot uniform with a bloody eye walked back towards the aft part of the plane with an axe in tow. For all they knew, this scene could have been straight out of a horror movie.

As Mitch reached the back of the rear lavatory, he unlatched the lavatory door and cocked his hand back with the axe held steady. He swung the axe, making a solid connection with the vanity wall, piercing through the flimsy plastic separators, allowing enough access to stick the nozzle into the hole.

Smoke filled the lavatory, which set off the smoke detector in the rear lavatory. A screaming, ear-piercing alarm caused nearby passengers to plug their ears.

"There's smoke in the bathroom!" a few passengers remarked.

Mitch took a couple more swings at the plastic until a decent-sized hole was produced. He grabbed the fire extinguisher, pulled the pin, and shoved the nozzle right into the hole, discharging the whole extinguisher bottle into the compartment where the black smoke was venting from.

Once the bottle was discharged and nothing more came out of the canister, Mitch grabbed the water extinguisher that was housed on one of the bulkheads and handed it to one of the passengers who had been sitting in the back of the airplane.

"Look at me," Mitch said sternly. "Look, if there is a fire again, I need you to keep on putting water and halon on it, long enough for me to land the plane. Okay?"

The eyes of the male passenger were wide, and he could barely grip the 20-pound canister. It barely seemed that he was understanding that there was a correlation between the smoke and the fire along with the hijacking. Nothing was really making sense for most of the passengers.

Mitch looked at the passenger, reassuring him, "All you do is twist this handle clockwise until you hear the CO_2 canister puncture and the handle will not turn any longer. Then, press this trigger and water will spray out. It has some good distance, so just aim it at the base of the fire. I need you to watch to see if there are any flare-ups while I go and land the jet," Mitch said.

Handing off the fire extinguisher to one of the passengers, Mitch marched his way forward to the flight deck, with all eyes of his passengers on him as he passed by. When he got to the flight deck, Wanda, shaky but determined, stood up and turned on the interphone in front of the passengers.

"The captain wants to know if there is anyone here who has flying experience," Wanda announced.

Wanda repeated the message along with telling the passengers to trigger the Flight Attendant Call button above their heads to alert her of the possibility of someone who could assist the captain.

A few moments of silence passed as Mitch plopped himself back into the left seat of the jet and tied himself into the harness and rested his headset back onto his head.

Suddenly, a quiet chime came from the cabin, and Mitch turned his head to see who had rang the flight attendant call button. In his haste, he noticed that the reinforced door was flopping around from the moderate turbulence. He had forgotten to latch it when he came back to the flight deck.

Mitch watched as Wanda carefully tried to balance herself in the turbulence, walk all the way back to row 13, and knelt down to meet the somewhat younger gentlemen.

A few moments passed as some words were exchanged, and Wanda stood up with a clean-cut guy.

The moments that it took for Wanda and the gentleman to walk up to the flight deck felt like forever, especially in the moderate turbulence.

"Mitch, this is Captain Derek, ah…" Wanda forgot his last name.

"No worries, Derek is okay for me. I'm an Air Force C-17 driver out of California," Derek introduced himself, extending his hand to Mitch.

Mitch's face lit up as Derek expressed his interest in trying to help a fellow pilot out.

"Please, come on in and sit down," Mitch said, "I'm fucking glad to see you!"

Mitch gave Derek a run-down on the layout of the simpler jet, in comparison to the large air force jet.

"Center, Eleven Seventy-two, we are with you," Mitch called out over the radio. There was still silence.

Mitch looked down at the radio panel. The knob that adjusted the volume for the radio. It was turned all the way down. Mitch pushed the recessed knob and it popped out of its recessed position, allowing him to turn the radio back up to an audible level.

"Center, Eleven Seventy-two? Can you hear us?" Mitch transmitted.

"Eleven Seventy-two, how do you hear center?" the controller replied.

Mitch looked at Derek, who was getting himself familiarized with the various buttons and functions of the jet.

"Center, we have you now. Must have hit the volume dial while maneuvering around the flight deck," Mitch radioed out.

"Captain, this is Hainsworth, glad to have you back with us," the Colonel replied over the radio. "What's your status?"

Mitch looked over at Derek again. "I have an air force pilot up here in the flight deck with me, the hijacker is dead, and we are back in control of the jet," Mitch announced.

"Thank God, we were seconds from having to make the decision to force you down," Hainsworth said somewhat shakily.

"Wh-What?" Mitch involuntarily shouted through the radio.

"We are coming up on your left wing now," Hainsworth replied. "We need to break off for fuel, and another escort should be on their way shortly."

Mitch felt a pain in his stomach, not realizing how close they came to actually being downed like how the Soviets did in the 1980's to the Korean Airlines jet.

Derek looked over at Mitch with a severely concerned look on his face.

"They were planning on shooting us down?" Derek asked.

Mitch didn't respond, except for a slight nod.

"Jesus fucking Christ!" Derek said, barely able to imagine that things could have gotten *even* worse.

A cold shiver ran down Mitch's back, as Derek's three words echoed in his mind.

Just as Mitch began dialing in a new frequency which had been given to them a few moments prior, a "ding" and a flashing yellow caution light on the dash of the jet flashed in both Mitch's and Derek's faces.

Mitch immediately pushed the caution button in, resetting it. He then glanced over to the display, studying it. The words "LO FUEL" had shown up, along with an indication on the fuel gauges turning yellow. This was a normal indication showing the aircraft was low on fuel.

"Well, we're only going to get one shot at this, so let's make it count," Mitch said while pointing to the display, which read the total amount of fuel onboard along with the current consumption rate of fuel.

Chapter 11
Nor'easter 1172, In flight,
09:55 a.m.

"Nor'easter Eleven Seventy-Two, Saint Louis Approach, descend and maintain five-thousand, you'll get vectors to the ILS runway One-Two Left," the approach controller announced.

"Down to five-thousand, we'll get vectors to runway one-two left, ah, Eleven Seventy-Two. Also, we are in a fuel emergency, so we will only have one shot at this," Derek replied, without confirming with Mitch.

Derek looked over and chuckled a nervous chuckle, "Sorry. Old habits, they die hard," Derek said smiling.

"No, quite alright, it's nice having someone who knows what they're doing," Mitch said smiling, finally allowing the weight of the past two hours lift off his shoulders.

The mental stress that Mitch had been under for the entirety of the flight was unbearable.

His girlfriend not only cheated on him, but with his first officer; being six miles above the earth during a hijacking; being escorted by the guy who ruined his chances at becoming a military fighter pilot and then nearly shooting them down; and now flying a damaged aircraft (with no gas) into a precision approach, with no way out.

Mitch inhaled and then exhaled before looking over at Derek.

"Okay, the big thing is that we need to make corrections for landing distances. The pages that I have are references of all the corrections that I need," Mitch said, pointing out the Quick Reference Handbook that was sitting on the dash, between both pilots.

"Easy. Give me two minutes, and I'll have them for you," Derek replied as he reached across the dash, gripping the spiral-bound book.

Mitch maneuvered the jet around as he was navigated by the controllers, setting up the instrument landing system frequencies along with the final courses, as prescribed by the procedures and the direction of the controllers.

Mitch plugged away at the flight management system, looking up occasionally to make sure that Derek could ask questions if he needed. Finally, Derek replied, "I've got your corrections here for you."

Mitch put up his hand, gesturing for the "one second" courtesy.

"Okay, give me just a second, I'll grab them here in a bit," Mitch said.

Mitch refocused onto the flight computer, which was the interface for all the aircraft functionality. He punched a few more items into the computer and then redirected his attention to Derek's calculations, which was a sheet of paper with a bunch of scribbling on it. The important thing was that Mitch could look at the final numbers, which were identified by a giant black box around the speeds.

"Okay," Derek said. "Based on our configuration, we will only have one shot at this, which we knew already. We have 9,000 feet of runway available to us, and we only need about 6,000 with our one engine. Reverse shouldn't be used, as it will promote non-uniform deceleration and unimproved directional control."

"Okay, I'd agree with you on that," Mitch said as he reached over to the center pedestal and placed his fingers on a metal toggle switch, which effectively unarmed the thrust reverser system for each engine.

"Okay, what else?" Mitch asked.

Derek also grabbed his weather corrections. "Okay, we are at minimums for a standard ILS, ceilings are 200 feet and visibility is variable at between a half and three quarters…"

"Fantastic, nothing like coming in under the wire!" Mitch joked, which made him feel somewhat better.

"Seriously, we may only have 600 pounds of gas left in the tanks when we touch down," Derek said with a concerned look.

"Par for the course my friend, let's get it in on the first try, then," Mitch joked again.

The tension was high in the flight deck as the two pilots continued to get the aircraft configured for the approach and subsequent landing. Something not adding up in the back of Mitch's mind. They were missing something.

Mitch rotated the knobs which turned on the intercom system, to which Wanda answered almost immediately.

"Get everyone ready for crash position. Evacuation is not likely unless we break apart. Emergency equipment will be waiting for us at the end of the runway," Mitch announced.

"Nor'easter Eleven Seventy-two, turn left to a heading of one-zero-zero, intercept the localizer for runway one-two left. Just to confirm, you are cleared for the approach," the approach controller said in a calm and soothing voice, as if nothing life-altering had just happened.

"Got it, one-zero-zero and intercept the localizer, Eleven Seventy-two," Derek replied, writing down the instructions on a piece of napkin, making sure that he didn't miss anything.

Derek looked over at Mitch. "They're worried about clearing us for the approach after all the shit we've been through?" Derek said with a slight chuckle of humor.

"Kind of funny, isn't it?" Mitch replied with a smirk.

"Yeah, I guess," Derek replied.

The jet rolled out on the one-zero-zero heading and Mitch stabilized the jet, heading directly towards the final approach fix, which is a pre-determined point in space used to navigate an airplane to the runway.

Mitch's head was outside of the jet, looking through the grey muck. "Okay, flaps twenty," Mitch called out.

Derek reached over to the flap handle and pulled it, but it was stuck. "Is there a trick to this?" Derek asked, unsure why the flaps handle wasn't moving.

"Oh yeah," Mitch chuckled. "Sorry. It's gated, so you have to push it down, then pull it to the flap setting you want, that'll move it."

Derek followed the instructions and pushed the handle down and pulled it to the 20° setting. The jet started buffeting and rocking a little as the shape of the wing changed with the deployment of the high lift devices.

Just as the flaps settled at their preassigned setting, the red and white overspeed indicator, commonly called the "barber pole" on the airspeed indicator, raced down to just above their actual airspeed. The jet began to pitch up slightly, which Mitch countered with a little trim, a tab on the tail which stabilized the airplane, and some forward pressure on the control column.

The speed started to decay, and the jet finally slowed enough to allow the next flap setting to be selected.

"Okay, Flaps thirty," Mitch called out, ensuring that the speed decayed enough so that he wouldn't get into an overstressed condition.

Derek moved the flap lever down to the next position, thirty, and waited. The outer marker beeped through the two pilots' headsets, which distracted Derek momentarily. "Final approach fix," Derek said.

Suddenly, a triple warning blurted out over the speaker along with another aural warning, "Flap disagree."

Mitch launched his eyes over to the display, losing his concentration on flying the jet and attempting to refocus it on the new problem that had just surfaced.

"Fucking great, our flaps are now jammed?" Mitch exclaimed, frustrated and done with the whole day.

The amount of frustration of the day's events lead up to this one point. It was the straw that broke the camels back. Mitch's veins bulged from his forehead as his rage and anger at life consumed him.

"God damnit, why don't we all just fucking crash and die. At least get it over with." Mitch said shaking his fists angerly at the gods.

"Never a dull moment…" Derek began in an attempt to lower the stress with a cheesy joke, but was interrupted.

Mitch closed his eyes and took a deep breath, still stressed and angered, "Bring the flaps lever back up and then reselect it again," Mitch said authoritatively.

Derek reached the flap selection handle and moved it back one position. The flaps started to move slowly before stopping again.

"They stopped moving in between. We are at Flaps twenty," Derek blurted out.

"Can anything else go fucking wrong?" Mitch shouted as he exhaled. "Take the QRH and look up that message. The Table of Contents is listed in order of severity, and then alphabetical within each section. Find the message and tell me how much more runway we need," Mitch said with an urgent tone in his voice.

"On it," Derek said, paging through the book as quickly as possible, trying to find the matching message.

After a few moments, Derek answered, "Okay, I got it."

"What does it say for calculations?" Mitch asked nervously.

"Well, first, we are ok with flaps twenty. Apparently, that's our normal configuration for a single-engine landing," Derek replied after glancing over at the checklist.

Derek grabbed the blank sheet of paper that he had been using for a bunch of numbers and jotted down the calculations. He then pulled out his cellphone and started to type in the numbers found in the book.

Derek looked up and glanced over to Mitch, with a puzzled look.

"What?" Mitch asked. "Talk to me."

"One second," Derek replied as he erased his writing and looked up the figures again.

Derek found the page again, wrote down the number that they had to multiply to get the corrected landing distance, and again completed the math.

"Shit, isn't this fucking fantastic?" Derek said softly, "We don't have enough runway, now it's saying we need at least 11,000 feet of runway… about a half mile more than what we have available to us."

Mitch rolled his eyes in disgust with respect to his fortune before exhaling, "Don't worry, we'll get her stopped one way or another. We don't have a choice in the matter," Mitch said as he called for gear to be lowered.

Derek reached over to the center pedestal and pulled the gear handle down, activating the display to develop more indications.

A few seconds passed as the gear was in transit. "Wouldn't it be funny if the landing gear failed, too?" Mitch asked sarcastically, but fully expecting the landing gear to not deploy.

A few seconds passed as Derek said, "Gear down and locked, you have three green."

"Thanks," Mitch replied rolling his eyes, secretly grateful for at least something working within the jet.

Mitch was handling the jet like a gentle hot rod, trying not to upset the natural balance of science and art, that was at play between man and machine.

The jet continued through the murky grey, and both pilots focused on their instruments.

"Runway in sight," Derek said as he squinted his eyes through the murky grey screen, his eyes fixating on two long rows of white lights and some flashing bluish hue lights leading to the runway centerline.

The ground proximity warning system chimed out, "Five-hundred," which alerted the crew that they were approaching minimums.

Mitch spoke up, "Five-hundred feet, we are stable, continuing."

"Is the first officer supposed to make that call?" Derek asked.

"Yeah, just trying to make it more of a routine landing, that's all," Mitch replied.

Mitch glanced down onto the audio panel and activated the public address system, shouting, "Brace, brace, brace!"

Almost immediately, Wanda could be heard on the other side of the door, shouting repeatedly, "Head down, stay down," as loud as possible.

Finally, when her voice couldn't keep up, she reached up to the interphone handpiece, pulled it down, and activated the public address system and again yelled, "Head down, stay down!"

Mitch transitioned his eyes, as he did several thousand times before, from looking at the instrument displays to the environment outside. Through the grey, he squeezed his eyes, and after a few seconds of looking, he could finally make out the faint runway approach lights, along with the red side row bars that looked like a giant red roman numeral two, and finally the runway edge lights.

"Got the runway in sight," Mitch announced loud enough for the cockpit voice recorder to pick up the callout. Just as the jet passed its final fictitious point in space, the jet called out, "Minimums."

The jet settled into a smooth descent rate as the turbulence became more and more dampened by the surface friction.

"One-hundred feet," the computer called out. Mitch pulled the thrust levers back, taking out the last little bit of power out as the jet settled into its final phase of flight.

Just as quickly as the turbulence left, a large gust of wind tossed the jet back up into the air higher. Mitch wrestled with the jet to regain control and salvage the *one* approach they had to get safely onto the ground.

"One hundred," the ground proximity warning system called out a second time. Mitch retracted the single working thrust lever back to its idle stop once again, ensuring that the jet had returned to stabilization. As the engine spooled down to the computer-controlled setting called "approach idle," the jet's speed started to decay as it settled into its final air segment, just above the runway threshold.

"Fifty," the proximity warning system called out.

"Over the threshold," Derek replied a little tense.

"Forty, thirty, twenty…." the computerized voice announced, which was Mitch's cue to begin pulling the nose up past the horizon. The aim was as close to the runway threshold as he possibly could, but still leaving a margin for error.

A short pause from the radio altimeter finally blurted out, "Ten."

Mitch pulled back the yoke a little more, bringing the nose of the jet a tad higher, and positioned the jet to land on the main landing gear as normal. The flair was significantly higher because of the lack of flaps, and the aerodynamic breaking allowed for the airspeed to decay even more before the main wheels touched the ground.

Mitch glanced out of the side of his peripheral vision, which showed the black asphalt screaming past him.

"We're floating!" Derek shouted.

"I know," Mitch said just as the main wheels kissed the pavement.

Mitch used a well-practiced motion to grab onto the speed brake's handle and rip it all the way to the deployed position, which deployed the speed brake panels on top of the wings.

"Fuck, we're still too fast," Mitch announced as he looked down at the thrust reverser arming toggle switches right next to him.

"Fuck it," Mitch grunted, as he grabbed the right metal lever and flipped it to the armed position, which armed the reverser system.

Reorienting his hand back to the operating thrust lever, Mitch grabbed the thrust reverser handle out of the stowed position, pressed the trigger with his middle finger, and waited for the computerized locks to release, allowing for the reversers to engage. Once they did, he yanked the thrust lever into the reverser mode, almost so violently that the metal scraping along his hand stung.

The engine spooled up and the jet lurched to the right, being overcompensated by the extra drag that was being produced by the right engine.

"L-look on the screen in the front and to the left. There's a green message, read them," Mitch said.

"Spoilers green," Derek replied before getting interrupted by Mitch again.

"Great, that's what I need, call out ninety knots," Mitch said again.

"Fuck, we're long," Mitch said again as he hammered onto the brakes after passing the two-thirds mark on the runway.

"Ninety knots, Captain," Derek called out.

A jolt and a muffled bang was heard within the cabin as both of the right tires blew out due to the over application of brakes. The jet violently veered off the right side of the runway.

"Fuck!" Derek called out.

"Hang on!" Mitch shouted as he shoved on the left rudder pedal, trying to regain control of the jet.

"Sixty knots," Derek managed to shout as he was being bounced around his seat.

"Oh fu…" Mitch's voice crackled as the right landing gear stub snagged dead-on to a drainage ditch opening, causing the jet to spin violently to the right.

The force of the impact shoved Mitch's head right into the side window, like the sounds of metal crinkling and crushing of an aluminum can.

A damp, warm breeze came over the two pilots within the flight deck. It was a sticky, humid air that laid heavily over the aircraft.

"Fuck," Derek heard Mitch proclaim along with the clear sounds of emergency equipment screaming towards the wreckage, their high-pitched screaming of their Oshkosh engines identifiable by the howling as the transmission shifted.

Mitch looked out the front window. The ground was not what he had expected.

The outside was orientated upside down. He was looking up at the ground and down towards the sky.

"You with me, Derek?" Mitch asked, looking over.

"So long as you can count that as your landing, and my takeoffs still equal my landings, I'm okay," Derek chuckled.

"Fair enough," Mitch said, wincing at the nice goose egg that suddenly formed on his forehead.

The force of the impact was so violent that it ripped the flight deck off from the rest of the fuselage. Debris flew in every direction as the main body of the jet spun around, the ripped hole facing the runway, which was filled by racing vehicles.

"One Hell of a landing, Captain," Derek laughed again, as he braced his hand against the ceiling, trying to cushion his fall. When he decided that it was time to stop hanging around, he twisted his quick-release harness that was keeping him tied tightly into the seat.

"Not a bad backup, yourself." Mitch chuckled.

"Is this a bad time to say I left training just before my check-ride, a couple years ago to fly heavies in the Air Force?" Derek replied, finally letting Mitch in on his little secret of being a previous airline trainee.

"Better than the alternatives, I guess," Mitch replied as he just hung, not really showing a sense of urgency in getting out of the flight deck. He really didn't want to deal with the mental stress of getting out of his seat right at this point in time.

Suddenly, a chirping sound came from a phone that had been lodged in the crew escape hatch handle, just above Mitch. He looked down, and it was Jim's cellphone that chirped loudly as the network connected and downloaded the updated content.

"Fucking Jim," Mitch muttered. Just as he said that, his cellphone buzzed as his cellular connection was also made with the cellular networks, processing the same data.

Mitch sighed loudly as he reached into his pants pocket and pulled out his phone and looked at the screen. It was a text message from Jenny.

"Well, I suppose, if I don't get down now, I'll have those rescuers groping me versus my passengers in no time," Mitch said as he put the phone back in his pocket without reading the content.

"Want some help, Captain?" Derek asked.

"No, I just have to think about how I'm going to get down from here without killing myself," Mitch chuckled.

Mitch braced elbows against the plastic coverings which made up the interior overhead panel and reached up to his harness, released, and twisted the handle.

Mitch plopped and slid onto the roof of the flight deck, which allowed him to pull himself back towards the circuit breaker panel and gain a foothold to stand up on his own two feet.

Mitch's phone chirped again as he looked at Derek. "You going to get that, Captain?"

Mitch shrugged and showed Derek the first line that was displayed on the lock screen of the phone.

"You'd be best if you were to read that now before all this commotion," Derek said, padding Mitch's shoulder.

Mitch nodded as he pulled the screen up, unlocking the message and reading the full content.

"Mitch, I know you're probably not going to read this until we part ways, but I need to tell you the truth as to what happened…"

The message continued, "Jim and I were on a trip a couple weeks ago. He was new and we hung out at the hotel bar where we had a few drinks."

Mitch closed his eyes and rubbed them with the side of his index fingers.

"Captain," a voice called out from outside of the wreckage.

Mitch was so absorbed in the message that he didn't hear fire rescue claw their way into the flight deck. Finally, Mitch felt a tug on his shoulder, which separated him from his hurting reality.

"Captain, you ready to come down from up there?" the man's voice said.

"Not really, but probably the best time is now," Mitch replied.

When he stood up on both feet and stabilized, Mitch reached over and grabbed Jim's phone and shoved it into his pocket before he was pulled out of the flight deck by the rescuers.

Within moments of the jet coming to rest, the Aircraft Rescue and Firefighting (ARFF) teams and vehicles rolled up on the wreckage of the jet. They arrived seeing the chaotic scene of passengers leaping over the four-over-wing emergency exits in an effort to get closer to the ground before they had to make the jump, since the jet was designed to be short enough that it didn't have slides attached to the exits.

Mitch looked out and around the wreckage of the flight deck and to the remainder of the fuselage, where he pinpointed Wanda, who stood in between the four over-wing exits, ensuring that all the passengers were able to deplane safely, shouting instructions.

The scene on the ground was chaotic, passengers used the last little bit of energy and mental effort to egress the now wrecked jet. They were running in every which way as fire rescue vehicles speeding around the airplane in an attempt to prevent any sort of fire from occurring.

When all the passengers exited from the airplane, Wanda turned around and hopped back into the aircraft and completed a quick walkthrough of the cabin.

The lights were beginning to dim due to the depletion of the self-contained battery packs. She checked each row to ensure that every passenger was able to get off the aircraft, and that there was no one left behind.

With rubbery legs, Wanda stepped up onto the wing of the fuselage as the flashing lights of the emergency vehicles mesmerized her. She took a knee and started bawling. Her gut was tied up in knots thinking she'd never see the ground alive or even another morning, given the past several hours of terror.

Wanda looked up with her eyes watering to find Mitch towering over her with a towel. As he helped her to her feet, he wrapped the towel around both of them. He put his arm around her fragile, vulnerable frame and began walking her down the wing to the ground.

"I'm going to look through the cabin," Mitch said as he ushered Wanda to one of the waiting ambulances.

"I already did, it's all clear," Wanda said, telling Mitch to go with her for medical attention.

The jet was mostly intact with the exception of the flight deck, which ripped off, creating a zipper effect of the metal around the curvature of the fuselage just before the galley, undoubtedly aided by the departure of the main cabin door in flight.

Mitch stopped about midway to the emergency equipment and turned around.

The passengers were being rounded up by the firefighters and police, making sure that everyone was accounted for and treated.

"I'll be right back," Mitch said to Wanda, giving her the towel that covered both of them.

Walking back to the aircraft, Mitch hopped into the emergency exit and entered the aisle, which was dimly lit by the fading emergency lights. In the aisle towards the back, Mitch stopped around row 13, where the flight crews normally put their bags when they were working a particular flight.

Seat 13B was relatively untouched through the entire ordeal. The seat location where all the crews kept their luggage. After grabbing Jenny's and his bag from the overhead, Mitch lifted the arm rest and sat down in the seat. He pulled out his phone again and opened the lock screen again to read the rest of the message.

"… Jim took advantage of me. He raped me."

The message continued, "I sent him a text message that I told you and HR about it…"

Mitch glanced over the message again, his eyes gravitating towards the words, "I forgive you."

The first time he read the message, it skipped over the final five words in the text.

"I will love you forever," it read.

Mitch sat back in the seat in silence again, deep in thought. He reached into his opposite pocket and pulled out Jim's phone and turned the screen on, a message being displayed on the lock screen from Jenny's message.

"I told Mitch and Human Resources about you. You ruined Mitch's and my relationship by you texting me like we were friends and lovers."

The text continued, "You took advantage of me, you raped me. Any amount of fake caring wouldn't change a thing. You are a pig."

Epilogue
A few months later
Ohio Western Reserve National Cemetery

The fall breeze blew across the headstones of countless simple white markers, showing a religious symbol of each of the fallen's faith, along with a name, branch, and finally, dates.

Mitch slowly stepped along the well-manicured grass, passing headstones of so many unknown veterans who lay beneath the surface. If there was one thing that Mitch understood, it was making sure to pay respects to all those who had died as he passed their gravestones.

While walking up and down the white markers, he came across a granite headstone with a name emblazoned on it that Mitch hadn't seen for some time.

"Hey, buddy," Mitch said to the headstone belonging to Charles Zerwas, his good friend who died in Afghanistan when their base came under rocket attack from the Taliban.

"A lot's been pretty fucked up," Mitch said, looking down at the dead grass clippings that accumulated near the headstone. Mitch reached down and started clearing some of the dead clippings off the grave area, cleaning it up and making it a bit more presentable.

"You know that girl that I was seeing? She's here too, a few rows over from you," Mitch said, glancing to where Jenny's marker was located.

"I don't quite know. I'm still in shock," Mitch teared up, looking around.

"You remember that one time, before you had left us, we found an old green rocket launcher tube that we had taken from an army guy who tried to smuggle it home?" Mitch chuckled. "We all pretended that it was the largest piece of male anatomy which required someone to shoulder mount in order to make it sit up straight? Like the photo from World War II?"

After a few minutes, Mitch got to his feet after sharing a couple fun stories from their memories together. He reached into his pocket and pulled out a quarter. Gently, he placed the quarter on the smooth, flat top of the headstone, making sure that it displayed proudly that his wingman was never forgotten.

Once Mitch finished his ritual with Zerwas, he walked over to the walking path, a few yards down, and made his way to Jenny's grave, which still looked fresh.

Mitch knelt down next to Jenny's grave marker, the lump in his throat becoming overbearing, and a warm tear rolling down his face.

"I'm so sorry, babe," Mitch said with his head hung low. "I'm sorry for what I said, and if only there was something that I could do to bring you back."

Mitch sat a few more minutes, talking to the gravestone, in which he looked over the finer details of the engravings. He picked the dust and dirt from the little crevices, making sure it was presented in a manner that everyone who passed would know she was loved and not forgotten.

Mitch reached into his pocket and he slowly pulled out his gift to Jenny and laid it on her headstone.

The diamond engagement ring sparkled under the partly cloudy skies.

"You were important to her," a voice said calmly behind Mitch, distracting him from his thoughts.

"Erik," Mitch said as he shot up to his feet. "I'm sorry, I didn't hear you coming."

"She would have made a nice wife to you. She always talked about you in such high regard. And, I never had known anyone to brighten her day like you," Erik, Jenny's father, said as he stepped in closer to Mitch.

"Thank you, sir," was all Mitch could say.

"You know something?" Erik said. "When you raise a child, especially a girl, you want to make sure that whomever she ends up with, that she is safe and happy. And I think you brought out both qualities in her."

Mitch's eyes swelled up, tears no longer being able to be held back.

"She was special," Mitch managed to say as his chin involuntarily shook, trying not to make eye contact with Jenny's father.

"I should go," Mitch said as he started taking a step or two, remembering to place a penny on the grave.

"I wish there was something more meaningful than a coin and her engagement ring that I could leave on her stone," Mitch said as he reached into his pocket, pulled out a penny, kissed it, and paid it on Jenny's headstone.

Later that day

"Mitch, you've been through a lot over the past six months. As part of your physical and mental preparedness to becoming a fighter pilot, we need to make sure you're in decent mental health," the doctor said, glancing over at Mitch and then back down at his piece of paper.

"You're hurting and I can tell that. How about you tell me what's on your mind?" the doctor nudged Mitch to open up.

Mitch sat in the chair and thought hard about the question posed to him.

"What is on my mind?" Mitch thought.

Finally, the doctor spoke up again.

"Look, I'll make a deal with you. You help me out with getting you checked out, and then I'll help you out in fulfilling your dreams as a fighter pilot."

Mitch's head jerked towards the doctor, and finally something made sense.

He exhaled and looked at the doctor again and opened his mouth, "Well..." Mitch stopped and looked blankly out the semi-transparent blinds again.

"After all that happened, the flashing lights, the photography, the interviews, the investigations, and all the so-called 'heroic' actions, it's just me. I'm alone," Mitch said.

"Okay, so, the plane landed roughly..." the doctor said before being interrupted.

"That's putting it mildly," Mitch said.

"Okay, the plane crashed, and you were found sobbing in one of the seats. It must have been a pretty profound experience, right?" the doctor asked.

"I guess you could say that," Mitch replied softly.

"Tell me more about what happened. What did you feel afterward?"

"Well," Mitch began. He recounted the feeling of emptiness and not being able to find the support structure. "It's like everyone knew my name and wanted to share a drink with me, the hero. I'm no hero. If I were, Jenny would still be alive..."

Mitch was interrupted by the doctor.

"If you were the 'hero' you thought you were, then the plane would have a lot more than just ten dead. Nobody would have been alive," the doctor said.

"No," Mitch countered the doctor, "there was an armed Air Marshal onboard my airplane. He was off-duty, traveling to meet his partner in St. Louis since his partner missed our flight. Why did he wait to step in until the very last second?! Jenny could still be alive as my WIFE right now!" Mitch exclaimed.

"Maybe he did was he was trained to do?" the doctor queried.

"No, I don't think so," Mitch replied softly.

"Okay, so the Federal Air Marshal, he's out of the picture. Why do you not think of yourself as a hero?"

"It's like you're on deployment. Your mission is right in front of you. You have an objective. You and your team members experience the same things that nobody else would experience. You needed one another. But now, everything seems so trivial," Mitch continued.

"If we didn't download the airplanes, the troops wouldn't get their meals, and the bullets wouldn't make their way to the war fighters. I remember watching a video of a girl bawling her eyes out and screaming because the presidential candidate whom she hated had won the election. I remember watching someone complaining online that they couldn't watch the royal wedding because she had to work. And we're out here putting dead bodies in aluminum cases, draped in the American flag, on an airplane, sending them home to a grieving family. It's all just so trivial in the grand scheme of things."

The doctor lowered his glasses and jotted down some notes.

"You know, Mitch, you have a perspective that many people don't understand," the doctor said. "You have the perspective of reality and what real humanity is."

"Maybe," Mitch replied.

"Maybe, Mitch, you need to find your next mission. Your next purpose. I see a lot of vets here who are struggling, like yourself, and they struggle because nothing in their lives or in our world can ever replace the brotherhood, the camaraderie, the experience, and the purpose."

Mitch glanced out of the window again.

"A purpose, you say?" Mitch replied, not completely convinced at the concept, but not totally opposed to it, either.

"You're a pilot. Find a volunteer organization to fly for when you finish pilot training," the doctor said with a slight smile on his face.

Mitch glanced out the window again, his hands reaching into his blazer, which Jenny had given him.

The doctor sat in silence, studying what Mitch was fishing out of his jacket.

Mitch retrieved a plain, unopened envelope from his coat pocket and glanced down at it before handing it to the doctor.

"This came this morning," Mitch said as he glanced back out of the window.

The envelope had the United States Air Force seal in the upper left corner, above the address box.

"So, why didn't you open it?" the doctor asked.

"I don't know. I made it to an E6, a Technical Sergeant. If this is a letter of rejection, do I still want to remain in the military? If this is a letter of acceptance, given everything that I've been through, is it worth me going to fly jets?" Mitch responded, somewhat pessimistically.

"I see," the doctor said. "Off the record, you would make a great pilot, I think. You will have a lot to learn, but it clears your slate into something bigger."

"On the record?" Mitch asked.

"On the record..." the doctor paused. "We would need to see what this letter says and make my determination. Right now, I cannot honestly say with 100% certainty that you aren't going to lose your mind."

"Well, open it, and let's find out," Mitch said as he pointed to the letter.

"Okay, do you want to?" the doctor asked.

Mitch shook his head. "No, you go ahead."

The doctor took his pen and casually slipped it in the little gap between the fold and the first layer of glue, pulling it in a controlled manner. Once the envelope was opened, the doctor cleared his throat and read the letter for himself.

"Well," the doctor began, "these are orders to attend Undergraduate Pilot Training (UPT) in Vance Air Force Base, Oklahoma."

Mitch sat quietly in his seat for a minute, digesting the new path that his life was about to take.

"I wish Jenny were here for this," Mitch said softly.

The doctor looked down at the set of orders and inhaled.

"I'm sure she's looking down upon you now, and will be your guiding star or angel, or both."

Letter from Tim

Dear Reader:

I want to personally thank you for taking time in reading my second novel. I do hope that you found an interest in this publication, and that you will be on the lookout for my future compositions.

The Union was an extremely fun novel to write, and I take great pride in its future, and I look forward to producing more advanced novels and books which bring the whole spectrum of a community together.

I wish you the best in reading this and future novels, and please, if you have any questions, or you just want to provide feedback on how my future novels can be improved, please feel free to contact me.

You can contact me via e-mail at:
Timwnordberg@gmail.com

Sincerely,
Tim W. Nordberg

About the Author

Tim was born and primarily raised in the Southwest Metro of Minneapolis, in a town named Shakopee. He graduated from Academy College of Aeronautics with a degree in Business Administration and a minor in Aviation Business. He currently puts his degree to use in a logistics and aviation role. He currently resides in the Twin Cities.

Contact the author:
Website: **timwnordberg.com**
Email: TimWNordberg@gmail.com
Facebook: **www.facebook.com/TimWNordberg**

Printed in Great Britain
by Amazon